Off-Limits

Copyright © 2025 Alexandra Louise

All rights reserved

Cover design by: Alexandra Louise

To all the girls who prefer the blonde guy. The dirtier the better…

Off-Limits

~ PROLOGUE ~

Jake

Three Years Ago

"Dude! What the fuck?!" Thatch called out to me from across the room. The party was loud, but he was louder. I knew I fucked up. I really fucked up. But I was hoping he would keep his cool about it. I backed away from the cause of him yelling profanities at me; his sister. "I'm going to kick your ass right now!"

"Okay, look," I started, backing away from him. "It was just a kiss and we're both drunk and, I get it, that's not an excuse, but I swear nothing more was going to happen."

That's not true, I probably would have fucked her if she let me, and he knew it too, hence the ass-kicking. But in my defence, we were both really drunk and I would never have even gone near his sister otherwise. She also came onto me, so...

"I don't care. That's my sister!" he yelled back.

"Hey," I looked over his shoulder to Olivia who was standing behind him, "you can jump in anytime and stop him." She just shrugged. She actually shrugged, as if she didn't care that her brother was about to punch me in the face.

"Don't talk to her," he said back to me. "I don't want to ever see you in the same room as her again."

"Dude, come on. It won't happen again. I swear. You're really going to punch me and have me look all fucked up for the game on Mond—"

And his fist made contact with my jaw.

Great.

~ 1 ~

Olivia

"Happy birthday, big bro!" I called out when Owen answered the door.

"Thanks," he said, pulling me into a hug.

"So, how's being thirty?"

"I don't know," he shrugged. "The same as twenty-nine, I guess. It doesn't feel much different."

"Well, that's good I suppose."

I headed into his massive 'baller NHL mansion', as my sister-in-law, Greya, liked to call it. Well, she wasn't exactly my sister-in-law. She and Owen weren't married yet, but she was pretty much already my sister. Owen was a big NHL star for Colorado, so their house definitely reflected it.

"Hey," Greya greeted me when I walked into the kitchen. She was just finishing plating some appetizers before the party. I had come early to help set up, but really it was just to hang out for a bit before more people showed up. I never really went to any of Owen's parties because they were full of NHL players I didn't care to associate with. But this was his birthday; the big three-oh. I was going to be there for this one.

"Need help with anything?" I offered.

"Nope, we're all good," she replied. She placed the tray on the expansive quartz centre island and headed to the living room with me. I sat down next to their cat, Stan— short for Stanuel. Yes, Stanuel. I mostly call him that to piss Owen off because he was Greya's cat first and his name was originally Stanley, but then when Owen pointed out it was like the Cup, Greya had to change it so it wouldn't be too hockey related (she was not a fan of hockey players at first, and honestly still isn't. I think the only one she likes is my brother). So now he's Stanuel and will forever be a Stanuel in my eyes.

"So, what's new with you?" Greya asked, sitting beside me, tucking her legs under her.

"Not much. My boss is still an asshole who never listens to my ideas, but if anyone else pitches the same thing, he's all over them."

"Ugh, why do you still work there?"

"Because if I want to get anywhere in marketing, he's the guy to learn from."

"Well, I don't think it's worth it if he basically ignores you. What exactly are you going to learn from a misogynistic prick?"

I shrugged. "I don't know, but for now, it is what it is."

"Yeah, Liv," added Owen, coming to sit with us. "You seriously need to start learning to stand up for yourself and say no to people."

"I can say no." I think. I mean, I could definitely see myself saying no to someone someday.

"No you can't. You're kind of a pushover, and I mean that in the most loving, brotherly way possible. You have to start learning to tell people off." I rolled my eyes at him. "It's like that time I got home from hockey practice to find you and two Mormons *praying* in the living room! Because you couldn't tell them to just go away!"

I winced and glanced over at Greya. "Okay, in my defence, one of them was kind of cute. But, okay. Whatever. I will try to start standing up for myself more," I answered, sticking my tongue out at him.

Then the doorbell rang and more guests started to arrive and my surroundings began to get increasingly louder.

Before long, Owen and Greya's house was packed. I mostly hung out with Greya and her friend Stella. Stella and her husband Gabe, my brother's best friend—or, best not hockey related friend—were going to have their second baby in a few months, so she was happily acting like a beached whale on the couch while he brought her food, and I was enjoying hanging out in the little bubble of not having to talk to too many people either. I looked up for a moment and it was like my eyes immediately homed in on him as if looking through a sniper rifle—which would be fitting considering my feelings toward him; Jake Ellis. The guy I kissed three years ago and the biggest mistake of my life. I was honestly surprised that Owen invited him tonight—or rather, both of us. We hadn't seen each other since the night of 'the incident', but we had certainly learned our lesson, and Owen had never brought it up again. Maybe he was starting to see that it was just a momentary blip in both of our lives and us being in proximity to one another wasn't going to have catastrophic results.

"I'm going to go get another drink. Want anything?" I offered Stella.

"I'm good for now. If I drink too much, I'll basically be living in the bathroom with how much I'll have to pee. Little man sure likes to use my bladder as a soccer ball," she said, rubbing her stomach. "Thanks though," she smiled.

I excused myself from the couch and headed to the kitchen where I poured myself a drink in one of those quintessential red Solo cups. You'd think multi-million dollar athletes would splurge for something classier, but I guess Solo cups had been serving the partying world for decades now and there was no need to improve on perfection. I was heading back to the safety of Stella, Greya, and the couch when I got stuck behind a group of people all insanely taller than me—hockey players—and there was no possibility of escape.

"Hey," a voice came from the massive chest in front of me.

I looked up at the man who the chest belonged to. "Hi," I replied, then paused. "You sure you want to risk talking to me? Does my brother know?" my eyes narrowed.

Jake just took a sip of his drink and swallowed. "It's been three years. I think he's over it."

"Maybe, but you never know. You don't usually forget something like that."

"Is that so?" he raised his brows. I didn't answer him. "Oh, come on. Don't act like you don't still think about it," he drawled with an air of seduction. Repulsive seduction; just to clarify. Was he even capable of saying anything without it sounding sexual?

"Yes, Owen kicking your ass after you stuck your tongue down my throat will forever be one of my fondest memories," I smiled.

"Hey, your tongue started it," he retorted.

"Maybe, but he never needs to know that."

"You like being a tease, don't you?" he smirked; that stupid grin that would have many other girls instantly weak at the knees. Not me, though. I saw right through it.

"I mean, it is kind of fun," I took a sip of my drink.

"Well, girl Thatch," said Jake, taking another sip of his drink. Then, like he was rethinking something, he paused. "Actually, scratch that," he shook his head. "That's what I call your brother, and that's just weird."

"You call him *girl Thatch?*"

"Haha, funny," he deadpanned, "but, no." Then he sighed, "Now I'm going to be forced to call you by your first name like a fucking loser. *Olivia,*" he added in a mocking tone. "Although," his brows raised, "I do like the sound of your name coming from my lips. *Olivia.* It's good, isn't it?

Bet you'd like it even better hearing me screa—fuck!" he groaned after I sucker-punched him in the gut.

See, Owen. I can stand up for myself. "See ya, Jake. Nice talking to you as always," I said after patting him on the shoulder as he was curled over.

"Did you just punch Jake?" asked Greya, coming up to me when I was back in the living room.

"Yeah," I answered nonchalantly.

"You want to tell me why?"

"It's Jake."

"Fair, but…" I walked past her and headed back to the couch. "Well, the good thing is, it doesn't look like Owen saw anything." She paused a moment. "But, you know…if you did like Jake and actually wanted to go there, I'd have your back. I can deal with Owen."

"What?" my head shot to her. "No, no, no. I was just really drunk the one time I kissed him three years ago and that was that. Jake's his friend; his teammate. That's even more sacred somehow, and I've learned my lesson. I'm not going there again."

"Okay," she shrugged.

"You sure?" interjected Stella. "I mean I get it. We've all had a crush on Jake Ellis at one point."

"What?" asked her husband, who had suddenly appeared beside her.

Stella looked up at Gabe and smiled, "I love you," and took the plate of snacks from his hand, then he headed back to Owen and the others.

"Um, yes. I'm positive," I assured her.

I managed to steer clear of Jake for the rest of the night.

When I headed home after I had reached my party quota to my little one-bedroom apartment, what Greya said had stuck with me. Not about Jake—*EWW*—but about my boss. Maybe it was time that I just found a new job with a boss who actually listened to my ideas. I had only graduated a few years ago, and this was the first real job I had managed to get in marketing. I didn't want to screw it up. So, I was going to put up with the asshole that was Carter Callaghan for the time being.

My weekend was still far from over the next day, and I used all of my Sunday to work on my pitch for Mr. Callaghan so that I would be ready for him bright and early Monday morning. That was how he liked it. He expected all of his employees to be in the office at least an hour before him and to hit the ground running, and more business lingo... *This was it.* It was finally my big shot at getting him to notice me.

Monday morning I was in the office bright and early, wearing a cute little work ensemble that said, *look at me. I'm exactly the type of person you want on this account.* I was prepping the conference room for my presentation when some of my co-workers started to file in. Most ignored me, staring at their phones, but the occasional one offered up a quick smile to acknowledge my presence. Then Callaghan walked in, all imposing and important. He took the seat at the head of the long table directly across from where I was standing. He was amongst the group that didn't even acknowledge me and just kept typing something out on his phone. When the room was full, I took a deep breath and started my presentation.

It did not go well. Well, it did, but Mr. Callaghan was on his phone the entire time, not paying attention to a word I had to say. When I was done, he looked up briefly and thanked me as if he was signalling me to go away, not because of the work I had actually done. There he sat in his cushy chair with his stupid, smug grin and receding hairline—yes, definitely receding hairline. He was the type of man who thought he was above everyone else and only did things that would benefit him. I'm not even sure how I got hired, to be honest. Maybe it was because HR told him he had to start hiring more women, or maybe it was because he didn't bother with anything to do with hiring. Either way, I stood there, silently packing up my presentation packets while he chatted with some of the other senior members of the team. All men.

"So, what are you thinking of this year's season?" began Henry, a senior marketing manager. He was exceptionally good at his job, and he was actually one of the few people who knew I existed.

"Ah, as long as Ellis can bring it this year, we'll be golden," Callaghan replied. My ears perked up at their conversation. Ellis? Were they talking about…hockey?

Wow, good to know my presentation really made an impression. I slowly walked over to them, pretending I was grabbing my other papers from their end of the table. "Sorry, are you guys talking about hockey?" I quietly asked.

"Yeah, why?" replied Brian. Fucking Brian. I hated him. He rarely gave me two glances and was Callaghan's little pet. I'm honestly surprised he answered me.

"Oh, no reason. I just heard you mention Ellis. Was wondering why?"

"Why? Because he's the best damn player on that team," replied Callaghan. Of course he would be a Jake Ellis fan.

I snorted inside my head. "I'm sorry. *Jake Ellis?*" I clarified.

"Yeah," replied Brian. They all stared at me for a moment as if they were looking for me to say more, or surprised I even knew the name in the first place.

"Sorry, I just…I know him. I saw him this weekend, actually."

"You know Jake Ellis?" Brian glared at me, utterly appalled by the notion. As if *I* could know someone like him.

"Yeah," I answered slowly, as if backstepping on what I had just said. "My brother is Owen Thatcher."

"No shit," called out Henry, leaning back in his chair.

Then Callaghan turned to me. I think this was the first time he had ever looked at me. It was unnerving and I noticed he had these dark, soulless eyes, which I would have never noticed previously, seeing as they have never made contact with mine before. "And you know Ellis?" I think those were the first words that man had ever said to me since I started working there six months ago.

"Yes. Um…he's my boyfriend, actually." *What? Where did that come from? Huh. So this is how all those girls in movies and books get into situations like this.* All the men couldn't take their eyes off of me as I smiled nervously.

"What was your name again? Ophelia?" asked Callaghan.

Wow. Impressive he even got the 'O' right. "Olivia. Thatcher. Olivia Thatcher. I mean, duh, my brother. Just Olivia is fine."

"Well, Olivia," began Callaghan. "Why don't you run over your pitch with me again? I'm afraid I had some important business to attend to and wasn't giving you my full attention."

Completely and utterly shocked!

Consider my flabbers ghasted.

By the end of the day, I was chatting with all the guys in the office and I was the most popular person there. Callaghan loved my pitch for the marketing campaign he was working on—duh, it was genius—and he even put me on the team with Henry.

"Hey, Olivia. Good work today," smiled Henry as he headed out of the office.

"Thanks," I smiled back.

"Oh, and feel free to bring your boyfriend to the company dinner on Saturday if he's free. I'm sure Callaghan, and the rest of us, would love to meet him."

Oh, shit.

***

Me: *Hey, I need your help with something and you CANNOT tell my brother.*

Greya: *Ooo, I'm in.*

Me: *I need Jake's number.*

Greya: *I'm intrigued. Go on...*

Me: *It's for a work thing. I need his help.*

Greya: *Alright, but I'm calling it right now. You two are going to fall in love and live happily ever after.*

Me: *Not likely.*

Greya: *We'll see *winky face emoji**

***

I texted Jake the next day before my lunch break.

Me: *Hey, it's Olivia Thatcher. I need to talk to you about something.*

Jake: *Now I know your brother did not give you my number.*

Me: *Greya did.*

Jake: *I always liked her. What do you need, GT?*

Me: *??*

Jake: *Girl Thatch. So what's up? You know this could be considered treason. Are you sure you want to take that risk?*

Me: *Yes. I'm desperate.*

Jake: *Really? I like the sound of that, but I also don't want to get punched by your brother again. Or you, for that matter.*

Me: *It's nothing like that. I don't want to sleep with you. I need your help with a work thing. You willing to meet me?*

Jake: *Sure. Where?*

Me: *Coffee? In an hour?*

Jake: *Who says I'm free right now?*

Me: *Well, I know you were just having lunch with my brother and you're done now seeing as he told Greya he's on his way home.*

Jake: *Look at you, Sherlock. Okay, where?*

~ 2 ~

Jake

"Hey man, you want to go grab something to eat?" asked Thatch after the gym while we were walking through the parking lot.

"Sure," I replied.

"Hey, so I've been meaning to say that you were pretty cool at my party last weekend. Thanks for staying away from my sister."

"Dude, that was three years ago, get over it." Honestly, I was kind of sick of hearing about it, but I get it.

If I had a little sister, I probably wouldn't want her fraternizing with someone like me either.

"Still, she's my baby sister and she's sweet and quiet and innocent and if you go near her again, I'll kill you."

"She's not *that* innocent," I grumbled slightly under my breath.

"Excuse me?"

Oh, shit. "No, I didn't mean anything like that. I swear." I ran a hand through my hair and blew out a breath. "I meant she sucker-punched me at your birthday, okay. And that's it. Honestly. That was the extent of our physical contact."

He gave a slight smirk. "And why did she feel the need to punch you? I mean I get the urge to punch you for no reason, but I doubt that's the case here."

"I don't know. Honestly, I bumped into her when I was getting another drink and we were just talking. I swear."

"Good. Because if you do have more contact with her, believe me, I'll be the next person to punch you and I probably won't stop there. And it's going to hurt a hell of a lot more coming from me."

"I don't know. She's pretty strong. I did not see that coming, bro. Who just punches someone out of the blue?"

"Well, her brother is a hockey player. I taught her well."

"Uh-huh," I grumbled again.

"So, I think you're paying for lunch is what I got out of this conversation?" he smirked as he unlocked his car.

"Yeah, fine."

***

I looked down at my phone when I was heading back to my car after lunch with Thatch and there was a number I didn't recognize texting me. Not the first time that had happened. I figured it was some girl texting me that I may have drunkenly given my number to and didn't remember. I pulled it up and—no fucking way. Thatch would kill me if he knew who I was texting right now, but my curiosity got the better of me. She needed some help with something and persuaded me to meet her for coffee.

I met Olivia an hour later at the coffee shop she chose. It was a small, quiet place that I would have never frequented on my own, so the chance of anyone seeing us was very slim. She was already there looking adorably sweet in a flowered blazer and pencil skirt; the way her legs crossed at her ankles under her chair as she gazed out the window. I know she's my best friend's little sister, but I couldn't help but notice her. I always noticed her. Just like when she walked into that party three years ago and came right up to me and started making-out with me. It took me a second to register who she was, but by the time I did, it was too late. I had kissed Thatch's sister and there was no going back from that. I had always wondered why she came right up to me that night and kissed me. But maybe some things I will never know the answers to.

"Hey," I smiled as I took the seat across from her.

"Hi," she smiled back. "Want something?"

"I'm fine. Just here to see what you could possibly need my help with."

"Okay, I guess I'll get straight to it then." She tucked a piece of caramel hair behind her ear. It was lighter than her brother's, but she definitely had the same blue eyes as him— although I had never found myself trying not to get lost in his. "My boss is a total asshole and I have been struggling with him for months at this job. He loves my ideas, but only when they come from one of the guys in the office."

"So why don't you quit? He sounds like a misogynistic prick."

"Huh, that's what Greya said. Anyway, I can't quit because he's the best in the industry and I want to succeed. You know a bit about wanting to succeed, right?"

She was driven. I liked that.

"Sure," I shrugged.

"Okay, so yesterday I heard him talking with the other guys at the office about the upcoming hockey season and you were mentioned. Apparently he loves you." I smiled. "And when I told him that I knew you, he suddenly started listening to me more, and..." she winced and leaned back in her chair, looking down at her hands cupped in her lap. "Long story short, I may have said that you're my boyfriend and that he could meet you at our next company dinner."

"What?" When did I end up in a fucking rom-com?

Her eyes shot up to meet mine. "Sorry."

I took a deep breath and sighed. "So you want me to be your fake boyfriend for this dinner then?"

"If you don't have anything else going on? I can say you're busy with training to get ready for the season or whatever you do in your downtime, but I think if you don't come to at least one thing, my boss will catch on."

"Okay, so say I come to this dinner thing and schmooze your boss for you. Then what? Is that it? Do I need to come to more things? If you say we broke up, will he go back to ignoring you?"

"I—I hadn't thought that far ahead." She bit her lower lip and it made my stomach tighten.

"Okay, well, let's figure this out then." I shifted in my seat. "I've got roughly two months before pre-season starts so I'm not as busy as I will be then. I can give you those two months of fake boyfriending and then we go our separate ways. I can even drop by your work once in a while and bring you coffee or something."

"Why would you do that?" she asked slowly with so much skepticism I was starting to wonder the same. "All I asked for was one dinner."

"Well, maybe I want something out of this deal too."

Her demeanour shifted. "What could you possibly want?"

Then I got a downright glorious idea. "You. Well, a date with you. After all of this, I get to take you on a real date."

She scoffed, "No."

"Why not?"

"Because I know you. I know your reputation and I'm not going to just be another one of your floosies."

"It's not like that." I leaned in and rested my forearms on the table. "Look, the way I see it, if your brother finds out about this, good luck convincing him it's all fake. He's going to kick my ass either way, so I may as well get something out of it."

"I'm not going to sleep with you," she sat back in her chair and crossed her arms against her chest.

"Didn't ask you to."

"Oh, please. I know where your *dates* lead. That's not me. You're with a new girl like, what? Every other day? I'm not getting anywhere near you or," she glanced down at my lap for a second, "that thing."

"Excuse me?" I shot back. "I'm clean, not that it's any of your business. Do you think I'd be stupid enough to jeopardize my health and my career?" I took a breath, "Look, if I wanted sex, I could get that. I just want a date." She stared at me for a moment, contemplating. "You could also just tell your boss to shove it and be done with the jerk. The choice is yours. But if you weren't such a goody-two-shoes, people pleaser, we wouldn't be in this situation."

"I am not!" she shot back.

"Oh, you are. Believe me, you're a good girl. You have it written *all* over you," I dragged my index finger up and down the space in front of her.

"Alright fine. We can make a deal. If we're going to do this, then we're going to do this right. For the two months that you're pretending to be my boyfriend, that means you're faithful to only me. No other girls, no hookups, nothing. If you can be a loyal boyfriend for those two months—which I highly doubt—then you can take me on a date."

Now I paused a moment, contemplating her offer. It's not like I couldn't go two months without sex, but was she really worth it? "Deal," I said, reaching a hand across the table for her. She took it in hers and we shook on it.

I guess I was Olivia Thatcher's boyfriend now.

Correction: fake boyfriend.

~ 3 ~

Olivia

I can't believe he agreed to it. I do have to go on a date with him after this, but let's face it, he's not going to make it two months without hooking up with someone, so I actually won't be going out with him. We might need to hammer down how I will actually know that he didn't go out with anyone though. He would for sure just say he didn't to get a date out of this. I didn't exactly think that part through.

Me: *Hey, so how will I know exactly that you kept your promise to be a faithful boyfriend? It's not like I'll know if you hook up with anyone. I'm just supposed to trust you?*

Jake: *I guess so, GT.*

Me: *We might have to re-think some things.*

Jake: *Look, I gave you my word. I won't sleep with anyone while we're doing this thing.*

Me: *I don't know. I might have to figure out a way to keep a better eye on you.*

Jake: *Well, you could move in with me. But that probably still won't work. I could always be banging at the girl's place.*

Me: **Eye roll emoji**

Jake: *Unless you follow me everywhere I go? Minus hockey stuff, of course, because of your brother.*

Me: *That sounds horrible.*

Jake: *Well, those are my solutions. You can move in with me or just trust me. Pick one.*

Me: *Fine. I guess I'll trust you for now.*

Jake: *Good girl.*

Me: *DON'T EVER SAY THAT TO ME AGAIN!*

Jake: *Sure thing, GT *winky face emoji**

I placed my phone back on my desk and tried to refocus on my work. Henry came over to my work station a few minutes later with some questions about the campaign we were working on. It was for some new clothing brand that made all their clothes from upcycling old ones, or fabric, or bedding, etc. They were actually pretty cool and they were already extremely trending in the social media world. They just needed a professional marketing campaign to take them to the next level.

"Hey, so is your boyfriend coming to the dinner on Saturday?"

"Yeah, he said he'll be there."

"Sweet." Henry leaned down over my desk a little. "Honestly, I'm pretty excited to meet him. Is it weird that I'm fangirling over him?"

"No," I shrugged. "I'm sure you wouldn't be the first guy to be afflicted by the Jake Ellis charm."

"Fair. And I'm also a little pissed that you're going to be Callaghan's new favourite, but what can you do," he shrugged.

"Well, he's excited to meet all of you guys too."

He smiled and headed back to his desk.

This was good. Everything was going to work out. I felt like the *Emily in Paris* of Denver. Far less glamorous, but still killing it in the marketing world. Yes, it was only because of Jake, but I was just using my resources to get where I wanted to be in life. There was nothing wrong with that. Right?

Jake: *782412*

Me: *What's this?*

Jake: *The code to my house. So you can check up on me whenever you want. I do walk around naked a lot though, so...up to you if you want to risk it *winky face emoji**

Me: **barfing emoji**

Me: *I don't need that. I can trust you. I think...*

Jake: *Of course you can, but it might come in handy at some point. You never know.*

Me: *When would I ever need to get into your place?*

Jake: *I don't know. When your mind is driving you crazy wondering if I'm walking around naked.*

Me: *You're incorrigible.*

Jake: *Thank you.*

Me: *Not a good thing.*

Jake: *Depends on how you look at it.*

Me: *Yeah, and did you have to just Google what that means?*

Jake: *Despite what you may think, GT, I am an educated man.*

Me: **Eye roll emoji**

Me: *Anyway, I have to get back to work and you're distracting me.*

Jake: *Oh, way to stroke my ego. I can distract you more if you want...*

Me: *I wish there was a middle finger emoji, but there isn't, so you'll have to just imagine it.*

Jake: *I can imagine a lot of things with your fingers.*

Me: *That's it! I'm calling this whole thing off.*

Me: *Oh, wait. I found it *three middle finger emojis**

Jake: *Fine. I'm sorry.*

Me: *WOW. Didn't think you could actually apologize to a woman.*

Jake: *Oh, I apologize to women all the time. Mostly about how I've now ruined other men for them once they've been with me.*

Me: *Second barfing emoji*

Jake: *Alright, but all joking aside, I do want to help you and that's what the code to my house was for. I'm not going to break our deal, I just wanted to show you that.*

Me: *Well, thank you. I guess in your weird backwards way, you're trying.*

Jake: *So…we're back on?*

I let out a heavy sigh.

Me: *Yeah, we're back on. Don't make me regret this!*

Jake: *Women never regret me *winky face emoji**

Me: *Third barfing emoji*

After work, I met with my friend Keira for happy hour. She was one of the other women in the office and we gravitated toward each other my first week there. She had only been there a month longer than me and was my age, so we clicked immediately.

"I'm sorry, did you say Jake Ellis? Girl, you are the girl who would totally sew book jackets for all the shirtless men on the covers of romance novels. You can't handle Jake Ellis."

I rolled my eyes and took a sip of my drink. "Yes I can. He's my brother's friend."

"Yeah, no. I've read this book. You can't do it."

"It's not that big of a deal. It's one dinner."

"That's how it always starts…" She took out her phone and started Googling him. "Okay, I'm not even a hockey fan and I know who he is. *Oh. Okay. Seriously?*" She flipped her phone to me so I could see the screen. "He did an underwear ad!" There he was, a very shirtless and very ripped Jake in tight black boxer briefs. "Maybe you can sew him a shirt too," she mocked, and the noises that came from her as she scrolled through more photos of him were something else. I finally snatched her phone from her hand and placed it on the table. "Okay, but I seriously need you to sleep with him," added Keira after a sip of her drink.

"No, I'm not going to sleep with him. He's just helping me out with my job and that's it," I replied. Truth be told, I hadn't ever slept with anyone, and I wasn't exactly broadcasting that to people. I just played along anytime the topic came up. It was amazing what you could get away with if you just smile and nod along and let other people talk about their sex lives. I know Keira was my best friend, but she didn't need to know everything about me. I guess at twenty-five, that was sort of late given whatever standards are put out there by society. I just give off the vibes that I'm reserved, but that doesn't necessarily mean I had never done it before. Keira knows I've had boyfriends in the past, so who's to say one of them didn't take my v-card?

"You're fake dating Jake Ellis. God, I wish I had your life. He is so hot."

I rolled my eyes. I guess he was good looking—fine, he was obviously good looking. I will admit that. I'm not blind. In-your-face attractiveness was what he was sporting. He had that dangerous, ruggedly handsome thing going on with his chiseled jaw hidden behind a light amount of stubble and dirty blonde hair. Everything about that man screamed dirty, and everything about me; did not. And he was tall. I remember having to stand on my tiptoes when I kissed him and he still had to lean down to me. But he was my brother's friend and teammate and I was not going there—for real, anyway.

"Well, I'll give you his number when I'm done. I'm sure he'll be happy for the hook-up."

"Really?" her eyes lit up like the fourth of freaking July.

I shrugged. "So, anything new with you?" I took a sip of my drink.

"Nope. Just the same old boring life. Work sucks and no prospects in the love department. I can't believe you also got that account with Henry. Brian is a tool and he never listens to my ideas. I'm just his little work monkey; typing presentations how he wants them." She took another sip of her drink, "So, why won't you sleep with him again?"

"Keira! Come on."

"No, you come on. You're young and hot. Live a little."

"No."

"Ugh, you're so boring. You're twenty-five. You're not dead. Bang the hockey Adonis," she dramatically, but quietly, slammed her fists on the table.

I chuckled. "I can't. My brother would kill him. I'm not joking."

"Only if he finds out," her brows wiggled suggestively.

"I'm not risking it."

"Ugh, you're such a good girl."

"Why do people keep calling me that?"

"Because you are one. You never do anything fun or impulsive."

"I did three years ago when I kissed him," I reminded her.

"Yeah, and that was the only thing you have ever done as far as I know."

I didn't have many good girl friends growing up and those I did have I lost touch with after high school. I made a few friends in college, but they were more only-at-school friends and I didn't see them much. Keira was my first real adult friend and she was great. There was something about her that when we met, we just knew we would be friends for a long time.

~ 4 ~

Jake

All week I was terrified that somehow Thatch would find out that I agreed to be Olivia's fake boyfriend. I half expected her to tell him because all of this was some sort of prank she was pulling on me. Anytime he texted me or said anything to me, I almost flinched out of fear that was my last day on earth.

It never happened though. I made it through the week without a single suspicion.

Olivia was at my place Saturday evening, because she insisted that she come over to make sure I looked presentable for her office party—as if I couldn't dress myself. I opened the door to find her standing in a white, skin tight cocktail dress.

"Fuck!" I gasped. "Sorry…You look great."

"Thanks," she deadpanned as she brushed past me into my foyer. She looked around. "Why is this place so dark?"

"It's not dark. It's moody, and I like it."

"You like dark grey walls? Don't you want a bit of colour in your life?"

"Nope."

"Whatever," she rolled her eyes. "So, your closet upstairs?"

"Where else would it be? But honestly, I can dress myself. Been doing it for years."

She headed for the stairs and took her heels off at the bottom and tossed them aside, then started climbing. "Well, it has to be believable that I'm your girlfriend and if I just roll the dice on what you're wearing tonight, people might think we're not actually together because why on earth would I have let you leave the house like that?"

"Seriously?"

"I have seen you before the games, though. You do manage to clean yourself up quite nicely. I think my favourite is that navy suit you have."

"You know what suits I have?" I asked from behind her, leaning forward to talk right into her ear.

"I've seen a lot of game interviews, Jake. Women notice these things. It has nothing to do with you specifically."

"Sure," I smirked. I led her to my room and walked into the closet. She glanced around for a moment, taking everything in—and judging. She always looked like she was judging me. "Well," I motioned to the clothing, "have at it, I guess."

She browsed for a few minutes like she was in a clothing store and then pulled a few things out and carried them over to my bed and laid them down on it. "Okay, start with this," she held up a pair of pants and a dress shirt.

"Fine," I said taking them. Then I lifted a hand behind my head and pulled off my shirt.

"What are you doing?" she asked.

"Changing. Like you asked me to."

"Can you go in the closet or something?"

"What? You've never been around a shirtless guy before? See you are a good girl," I smirked. "Face it. You can't even fathom being in the same room as a half-naked man. Don't worry, honey. I won't show you the goods. Unless you ask nicely." She just rolled her eyes at me then turned around. "Okay, you can turn around now," I called when I was done changing.

"Hmm," she lowered a hip and leaned to the side with her hand on it. "No, try that shirt," she pointed to a blue one on the bed. It took four combos for her to finally decide on one; that navy suit she loved with a steel grey dress shirt and no tie. "There, now you look like you could be my boyfriend," she said walking slowly toward me. "You just need to tuck in the shirt." She grabbed the waist of my pants and shoved her hand and the shirt into them.

I didn't move. This wasn't my first rodeo. "You were hoping I'd flinch, weren't you?"

She looked up at me, her hand still dangerously close to something. "Well, I figured you would."

"Nah, you can put your hand down my pants as much as you want, princess. Doesn't bother me."

She started lowering her hand and—I flinched. *Slightly.*

She just smirked. "Maybe it does. And see, I'm not that much of a good girl." Then she turned and walked out of the room.

Fuck. That girl. It might be harder than I thought to keep my hands off of her. Something else was definitely harder too, so I waited a moment before joining her downstairs.

She was in the kitchen when I walked in. She glanced at me and smiled. "Why is there barely any food in your house?" she asked. "I wanted a glass of water and your fridge is basically empty."

"Sampson must not have gone shopping yet," I replied.

"Who the fuck is Sampson?"

"Wow, language, good girl." She glared at me. "He's my personal chef. He shops and cooks."

She scoffed, "Of course you have a personal chef."

"Duh, I don't like cooking. I gave him the night off because I'm going to dinner with you."

"Whatever. We should get going," she said heading to the door.

"Where are you going?" I asked. "The garage is this way," I pointed.

"To my car."

"No, we're taking my car."

"Why?"

"Don't you want to impress your boss? You think he's going to believe that I let you drive me around in whatever hatchback, girl thing you drive. No. Come this way." I led her to the garage and opened the door. There she was; my pride and joy.

"I'm not riding in that with you," she crossed her arms and tapped her foot in an obnoxious, but very hot, way.

"Why not?" I glared back at her.

"It looks like the Batmobile, and I don't trust your driving. I'm not going to get into an accident and then Owen will definitely find out we were together. Although, the accident might seriously maim you, so…I guess it's a win for everyone."

Breathe. Just breathe. Just take a deep breath. When I succeed in this little arrangement of ours and I get to take her on a date, it will have been worth it. Will it though? Yes. The answer is yes. Proving a woman wrong is always worth it. "That's it," I bent to her waist and grabbed her and threw her over my shoulder and carried her to the car.

"What are you doing?" she pounded at my back.

I placed her nicely down in front of the passenger door and opened it for her. "Get in, smartass."

***

When we walked into the restaurant, the whole place had been booked for the private event. I wasn't a stranger to fancy events; I've had my fair share of them, but this one was one of the nicer ones. Whatever company Olivia worked for was definitely raking in the big bucks. I knew she was in some sort of marketing, but that was about it. We were led to the rooftop patio where the rest of Olivia's co-workers were already there mingling. She had told me this wasn't just an office event, but it was networking for their firm also, so there were a lot of people there tonight that were potential clients.

"You ready for this?" I whispered in her ear right before we stepped onto the patio.

"Yeah, why?"

"Just wait." We walked into the room and as if a switch was flipped, all eyes slowly started following us.

"Oh for God's sake," whispered Olivia. "This is what it's like being with you?"

"Get used to it, baby doll," I said taking her hand and leading her into the party.

"I have a new respect for Greya," she whispered.

"Nah, Thatch doesn't draw this much attention. So," I turned to her, "where's the asshole boss?" She scanned the room for a moment and then spotted him. He was an older man, in his fifties or sixties. He definitely looked the part of misogynistic prick. She led me that way and when we got closer, he noticed us.

"Olivia," he held his hands out, "I'm so glad you could make it. And this must be the boyfriend?"

"Yes. Mr. Callaghan, this is Jake. Jake, my boss, Carter Callaghan." I took his hand and shook it. He was about the same height as me, and I wasn't a short guy by any definition of the word. He had a nice head of hair for his age too; a definite silver fox, so I'm sure that played into his superiority complex well.

"It's very nice to meet you, son," he said to me. "This girl of yours is a huge asset to our company," he motioned to Olivia, bullshitting to the max.

"It's nice to finally meet the man who has been taking all of Liv's time away from me for the last few months. She is a workaholic, this one," I wrapped an arm around her shoulder and gave it a little squeeze.

"That she is, and that's why we love her."

"Well, don't we all," I shot her an ever-so-charming smile. "But seriously, you're going to have to cut her workload back. It's almost pre-season and I'm going to have even less time with her then."

"Yes. I'm hoping this is our year," he added.

"Well, I hope that every year, but this one might just be it. You know, I have the love of my life, all I need is the Cup to make it the best year ever."

Alright, I may have been laying it on a little thick for this guy, but he was the epitome of stereotypical chauvinistic male that thinks women are beneath him. I honestly couldn't believe Olivia worked for that guy. If she actually was my girlfriend, there was no way I would encourage that. I mean, she was her own person and could make her own decisions, but that guy was not going to get her anywhere in life. I was starting to realize we might have to be fake together forever though, because he was definitely the type of grade-A asshole that would penalize her if we ever fake broke up. I stood there for a while longer listening to him talk up Olivia and give me every line about her I would want to hear, and I threw them right back at him. By the end of our conversation, that guy was eating out of the palm of my hand. He left to talk to some prospective clients, but I knew he was going to come back soon enough with them and use me to try to entice them to work with him. I didn't feel great about that level of exploitation, but it was for Olivia and she seemed happy.

"So, how am I doing?" I asked her when we had a moment alone at the bar.

"Great. My boss loves you, and me, and I think I may have convinced that client over there to sign with us."

"Hey," I smiled and gave her a playful punch on the arm. "See, look at you go. But I'm not convinced it's just because of me. I'm sure you would have bagged that deal without me being around."

"Maybe," she sighed, "but Callaghan wouldn't have noticed or appreciated it as much without you here."

"Well, as long as you're happy, I guess."

"I am. Thanks again for this."

"No problem."

"You are very good at fake boyfriending, though. You've never done this before?" she mocked.

"Why is it so hard to believe that I could be a good boyfriend?"

She looked me up and down. "Because you're you."

"Gee, thanks."

"I didn't mean that in a bad way. You just don't exactly scream boyfriend material," she gave me a halfhearted smile.

"Well, everyone out there is believing it," I subtly nodded to the crowd.

"True. Maybe you are made of a little more than I thought."

"Wow, high praise coming from you."

She rolled her eyes. I was starting to like the way she did that.

"Oh my God," interrupted this new girl coming up to the other side of Olivia. "You guys are *selling* it."

Olivia turned to me, "This is Keira. She works with me and is basically my best friend. We're both victims of this workplace, and we have to stick together. And she obviously knows about the whole fake boyfriend thing."

I smiled at Keira and held my hand out for her. She was pretty—not going to lie. I recognize a beautiful woman when I see one. She had tan skin and this dark wavy hair. Nothing compared to Olivia though, if you want my personal opinion. "Nice to meet you," I added.

"You too. You're just as good looking in person," she added.

"Happy to not disappoint," I smiled again.

Then she turned back to Olivia, "But seriously, everyone is talking about you two and Callaghan has this evil genius look about him. I'm not sure if it's a good thing, but I basically can't walk around this room without hearing your name."

"Well, let's hope it's all good talk then," Olivia smiled at her.

***

When we got back to my place, we sat in the car for a moment. Olivia was quiet the whole ride back and she seemed like she had something she wanted to say, but I didn't want to pry. "Well, I guess this is it then," I began. "Let me know when you need me to play boyfriend next," I added unbuckling my seatbelt.

"Can I ask you something?" she began. I nodded. "Why did you never tell my brother it was me that kissed you? You just let him believe that you were the bad guy that took advantage of his little sister. Why?"

I shrugged. "I guess I figured it didn't matter. He was going to blame me regardless and I was already signed up for an ass-kicking. You're his sister and he loves you. You can't do anything wrong in his eyes. You're a perfect little innocent angel as far as he is concerned and I guess I didn't want him thinking any less of you."

She didn't say anything, then finally, "Okay. Thanks again." She smiled and unbuckled too, then opened the car door. She took off my jacket I had given her before we left the restaurant because she was cold and handed it over to me. "I guess I'll see you later," she waved as she headed out of the garage and down the driveway to her car.

"Wait," I called, jumping out of the car and jogging after her.

"What?" she asked, turning to meet me.

"Nothing, just figured I'd walk you to your car. You know, like the gentleman that I am." She raised her brows at me. "What?"

"Whatever," she sighed. "Well, I'm at my car so you can go inside now." She unlocked her door—with the *actual* key. I haven't seen that done since I was a kid.

"Jesus, Olivia, how old is this car?"

"What's wrong with it? It's fine."

"I guess. Don't you worry about it breaking down? I have a hard time believing your brother doesn't have a problem with you driving around in this death trap."

"He…might. He has offered to buy me a new one but I refuse. I like Gretchen."

"Gretchen?"

"Yeah," she crossed her arms over her chest.

"That's the least sexy car name I've ever heard."

"Well, it suits her."

"You can say that again."

"Whatever." She pulled open the door and got in. "Goodnight Jake." She tried to start it and as if the universe was on my side, Gretchen didn't want to turn over—not surprising from a chick named *Gretchen*. Olivia sighed and tried again and on the third time, it started. "See, everything's good," she smirked at me.

"I guess so. At least think about letting your brother buy you a new car. It's nothing for him and when winter hits I don't need to hear about you freezing to death because your car wouldn't start."

"Aww, would you miss me?" she teased.

"Nope. Just don't need our *second* best player out for the season because of how distraught he'll be."

She rolled her eyes at me and put her car in drive. "See ya later," she waved as she pulled out of my driveway.

~ 5 ~

Olivia

The marketing event on Saturday was a huge success. We got three new clients and I was assigned one of the biggest ones. Everyone was talking about Jake and me on Monday morning and how we seemed like 'such a cute couple'. I guess we did fool everyone.

Me: *Oh my God, everyone in my office won't stop talking about you. I'm starting to regret this.*

Jake: *Ah, come on. You love it.*

Me: *Maybe.*

Jake: *You want me to stop by sometime this week?*

Me: *No, I think it'll be okay. I don't need you around too much. Maybe next week, though.*

Jake: *Just tell me when and where.*

Me: *Thanks.*

"Talking to *Jake?*" asked Keira, sitting down across from me at our usual after work drink spot.

I gave her a blank, unimpressed stare. "Maybe, but don't read into it."

"Uh-huh. Anyway, I hope you can keep up with all of this because everyone is talking about him and how you're Callaghan's new favourite. Man, I wish I had thought about the whole fake boyfriend thing first."

"Well, like I said. You can have him after me and then you'll be the new favourite. Or maybe he can set you up with someone else on the team."

"Yeah, we can start a business of hiring out hot hockey players to be people's fake dates to get ahead at work," she mocked.

"Anyway, I do actually have a lot of work to do. While I'm really happy to be noticed now, my workload has doubled and everything has to be even more perfect than it was before."

"Does it though? Honestly, I think you could do nothing and Callaghan would still be impressed. He's totally changed around you now, and kind of the whole office. He even said good morning to me today."

"Whoa, that's weird." I shrugged it off though. "I guess meeting his favourite hockey player put him in a good mood."

"Or maybe the fact that he thinks he can now interact with him more often is putting him in a good mood."

"Well, whatever it is, I'll take it," I added. "I'm getting even more praise and I think I might even be on track for a promotion."

"God, men are so stupid," she rolled her eyes.

I laughed. "Cheers to that," I said holding up my drink to her.

"So are you really going to keep this going for the next couple of months?" she asked.

"I think so. That was the deal. Once hockey season starts, Jake will be busier, so it won't be weird that he can't come with me to events anymore. Hopefully I'll be able to keep killing it at work, and he will be able to just slowly fade out of my life."

***

The next weekend, I was heading out of my appointment at this fancy spa downtown. It wasn't normally the type of place I would ever go to but Owen got me a rather large gift card for my birthday last year—and yes, I still hadn't used it all up yet—so I wasn't going to let it go to waste, and after all of my hard work at the office I decided I deserved a little pampering. Well, the massage was pampering, but the leg waxing I decided to add on was slightly less relaxing. It seemed like a good idea at the time and future me will appreciate it. *Curse my Mediterranean heritage.*

I headed for my car and prayed that it would start. Jake was right—as much as I hated to admit it—Gretchen had been more finicky than usual lately and that was one more thing that I really didn't need right now.

Of course she didn't start. Now what? I don't know why I chose to text who I ended up texting. There were a multitude of people I could have asked for help, but most of them would have berated me for not getting a new car sooner and that this was bound to happen. I wasn't in the mood for that.

Me: *My car won't start.*

A few minutes later, I got a response.

Jake: *And why are you texting me about it?*

Me: *Because if I text my brother, this will be the last straw and he will buy me a new one and I really don't want him to.*

Jake: *Would it really be that bad? I'd take a free car.*

Me: *It's the principle of it. I'm a grown woman who can buy things for herself. It's fine, I've been meaning to find a new one and I have a bit saved. It's just earlier than I thought it would be.*

Jake: *Suit yourself.*

Jake: *But back to why you're texting me. Are you stuck somewhere?*

Me: *Yes.*

Jake: *Where are you?*

Me: *At a spa downtown.*

Jake: *Do you need me to come and rescue you?*

Me: *You're not my knight in shining armour.*

Jake: *I could be. Just for today. If you ask nicely…*

Me: **Five middle finger emojis**

Jake: *You're getting good at that.*

Me: *Fine. Can you please come and help me?*

Jake: *Be there in twenty *smiley face emoji**

Twenty minutes later, just like he said, Jake had found me and was boosting my car. It still wouldn't start though.

"It's not your battery. I think this thing has just finally had enough of its miserable existence and died."

"Great," I rolled my eyes, leaning my butt against the side of the front bumper.

"It's going to need to be towed out of here."

"Great again. How much is that going to cost me?" I said more to myself than him.

"Don't worry about it. I got you."

"You don't have to."

He shrugged, "It's nothing."

He arranged the tow truck for me and it was rather awkward while we were waiting for it in his car.

"Why are you sitting weird?" he finally broke the silence and looked over at me.

"Huh?" I glanced back at him.

"You're being weird. Like you don't really want to *sit* on the seat."

I was slightly trying not to press my thighs against the seat. I'm not sure how I was planning on driving home if I was this uncomfortable.

"Oh, uh…no, I'm fine. I just got my legs waxed and they're a little sore." Add this to the list of super awkward and embarrassing conversations I never thought I'd have with Jake Ellis.

"Why would you do that then? If you're this uncomfortable after?"

"Oh, it's really not that bad and it goes away in an hour or so."

"Whatever." There was another awkward silence until he broke it again. "You know guys don't really care about that stuff, right? I mean, don't get me wrong, it's nice, some sexy, smooth legs, but it's not a deal breaker or a turn off. If a guy ever tells you it is, he's a *boy* and needs to grow up."

"I know. It's more for me. I like to feel sexy."

"Well good then. As long as it's for you."

"Well it's certainly not for you," I glanced over at him.

"All I'm saying is no one likes a hairless cat. They're weird and go against nature."

What? Oh, thank God the tow truck pulled up at that moment.

Jake was super nice when the tow truck driver showed up and fawned over him. He signed things and took a picture with him and I watched as he loved every minute of it. I gathered my things from my car and said my goodbyes. Gretchen was good to me for the years I had her, but it was time to move on. I didn't exactly know how I would get to work and things until I found a new one, but I would figure that out later.

"Why are we at your house?" I asked Jake when he pulled into the driveway of his stupidly over-the-top abode. Now that was what Greya would call a 'baller NHL mansion'. Honestly, theirs was pretty normal compared to Jake's place. I'm pretty sure he must have someone come out and vacuum his driveway, or something, because it always looked immaculate.

"Because I'm going home."

"I thought you were dropping me off?"

"Nope, you're dropping me off. You can take my car until you have a new one."

"Jake!" I turned to him. "I can't do that. There is no way I am driving this thing and it probably costs more money than I will ever see in my entire life."

"You can, and it's fine. If you don't want this one, you can have your pick of one of my other ones, but I'm not letting you leave here without knowing you have a safe way to get around."

I glanced over at him in the driver's seat. He was serious. "Okay…" I hesitantly replied. "Can you give me your least expensive one?"

He let out a small chuckle, "Sure."

I made it home having only a mild panic attack the whole way, making sure not to total Jake's car, but I managed to get it safely into my parking garage without a scratch on it. I was still incredibly nervous about driving that thing around, but it was saving me having to rent a car or take the bus until I could find a new one. Taking the bus to work wouldn't be that bad though, but it was really nice of Jake to loan me one of his cars. I guess he does have five, so he really didn't care about losing one for a week or so. Hopefully it was only a week and I could find a new one soon. I was already looking at used cars on Marketplace and I found a few contenders I was planning on looking at. I should probably ask my brother to go with me while looking, but he would just insist on buying me a new car and I was kind of hoping to do all of this without him knowing. I loved that Owen wanted to take care of everyone in his life, but I didn't need to ride through life being Owen Thatcher's little sister.

Maybe I could ask Jake? Would that be weird though? Would the sellers think it was completely insane that Jake Ellis was helping a girl look at used cars when he could easily also buy me one? I guess I could decide later. I could always ask Keira to help me. Her dad was a mechanic and she knew a thing or two about cars—oh, I just got the hairless cat comment. *Well, mine's not. Not that Jake Ellis will ever know that!*

Wednesday evening rolled around and I was actually going on a date. I met this guy on an app that Keira insisted on downloading onto my phone; *Drill-it* or something to that effect, and while I was not the dating app type of person, I still perused the available men in my area whenever I was curious and Nathan caught my attention. He was nice and made me laugh within the first few messages we sent to one another. We decided to meet mid-week so there were no assumptions of anything, seeing as we both had to work the next day.

I was really enjoying my time with him until his attention seemed to be drawn elsewhere for a moment. I looked in the direction he was looking in and—*ah, crap*; my brother. He was with Greya, and a moment later Jake walked in behind them. *Seriously?*

"Sorry," Nathan turned back to me. "I'm pretty sure I just saw Owen Thatcher and he's my favourite hockey player, but I'm here with you, so you have my full attention again," he smiled.

"It's okay, I get it."

"You a hockey fan?" he asked.

"Um, sort of. Want to meet him?"

"What?" He looked taken aback.

"Hang on," I smiled at him and then got up. I walked over to where Owen was and he saw me.

"Hey. What are you doing here?" he asked, pulling me into a hug.

67

"Um, a date, actually."

"What?" he instantly started scanning the bar for someone who looked like he might be waiting for his date to come back.

"Don't. Don't go all big brothery and weird. Anyway, he saw you and you're apparently his favourite player so…" I motioned to him.

"Alright, let's go," he smiled, and followed me back to my table, not before I caught a glimpse of Jake's expression when he had heard I was on a date.

"Owen, this is Nathan," I began as I was sitting back down and Owen took the empty spot beside me. "Nathan, this is my brother Owen."

"Your brother? Wow, oh, okay," replied Nathan.

"So," began Owen with all manner of seriousness and slight intimidation. "You're dating my sister?"

"Stop it!" I backhand slapped him across his chest.

"Ow! Okay, fine. I'm just kidding, man. It's nice to meet you."

"Yeah, you too," replied Nathan.

They talked for a few minutes about hockey and stuff and my phone was buzzing like crazy in my pocket with all the messages from Jake coming in.

Jake: *You're on a date? How come you're allowed to date and I'm not? Seems pretty hypocritical.*

Jake: *This is what the leg waxing was for, wasn't it? You better not have sex with him in my car.*

As much of an f-you as that would be; *I will not.*

Jake: *And how come he doesn't want to talk to me too? Clearly he has no taste and you shouldn't let this go any further.*

"I'm just going to go to the bathroom quickly," I interrupted Nathan and Owen as I stood and headed across the bar.

Me: *Will you stop! This is none of your business. It's not my fault you didn't think of this when we made our little arrangement. If you didn't want me going out with anyone else either, then you should have said something. So, sucks to suck.*

Jake: *Sucks to suck?*

Me: *Yes.*

Me: *And clearly he has excellent taste if he's going out with me.*

Jake: *Well, I guess I can't argue there.*

"Yo, coming in." My head shot to the bathroom door as I heard a familiar male voice call out from the other side. A second later, Jake walked in.

"Hey! What are you doing?!" I whisper yelled at him. Not that there was anyone around, but I didn't need anyone on the other side of the door hearing.

"Relax. Is there anyone else in here?"

"No."

"Then it's fine."

"No, get out! You can't be in here."

"Chill, will you." He turned to the door and locked it. "Not my first time locking the ladies' room at a bar."

"See, and that is the type of thing I just don't want to know." I leaned against the counter and crossed my arms against my chest. We stared at each other for a moment that felt far too long. "Well, this has been a pleasure, as always, but I have to get back to my date." I moved to stand straighter when he started walking closer to me.

"If you want to call it that."

"What?" I asked him.

"Your *date*. Doesn't seem very date like to take someone to a bar on a Wednesday evening."

"Well, that's what we decided because we're both busy with work. Who cares? A date can be whatever you want it to be. God, why am I defending myself to you?" I shoved past him and moved to head out when his hand caught my wrist and he pulled me back.

"I don't know. Maybe there's a small part of you that cares what I think."

"And what do you think?" I stood my ground and sized him up.

"I think that guy's not right for you."

"Excuse me?" I squared myself to him. "You don't even know him. And how would you know who's right for me or what I want?"

"Just do."

"And what makes you think you know what type of guy I want?"

"Well, I might not know the type of guy you want, but I know the type of guy you need."

So. Fucking. Arrogant.

"Oh, well please, enlighten me then," I motioned to him.

"Okay." He cleared his throat and took another step closer to me, backing me against the counter. "You need the type of guy who will be in your corner no matter what. The type of guy who will consider you the best thing to ever happen to him. The type of guy that will encourage you to stand up for what you want out of life, and will go along for the ride." He kept inching closer to me with every painfully poignant new thing he was listing, and my heart began pounding harder and harder with every step he took until I felt the hard edge of the quartz counter hitting my tailbone. He didn't stop though. "You need the type of guy who doesn't give a damn who your brother is because all he sees is you, and the type of guy that wants you as a partner in life because every moment you're in his, you make it all the better." He was a whisper away from me now and I could feel his warmth radiating onto me as my breathing was becoming heavier and heavier. He continued in a low, panty-melting voice, "He needs to know that you're the only woman capable of bringing him to his knees and the only woman whose air he breathes." He paused again; the both of us locked in a staring contest that I was terrified might only end with his lips on mine. He leaned in even closer—not that it was even possible based on how close we were already—and drew his gaze to my lips, his thumb and forefinger gripping my chin delicately. "Is he that guy?"

I sucked in a deep breath and blew it out, slightly quivering as I did. Then I somehow managed to compose myself from the Greek god of a man whose lips were inches from mine. "I don't know. But I'm not going to be able to find out if you don't let me leave this bathroom." I pushed him away from me and headed for the door. I unlocked it to find Greya on the other side.

"Having fun in there?" she asked with a wry smile.

I just gave her an exasperated glare and brushed past her. When I got back to my table, only Nathan was there.

"Hey," he smiled at the sight of me. "Thanks for introducing me to your brother. His fiancée pulled him away not too long ago so we could get back to our date. I hope you didn't feel like I was ignoring you?"

"Oh, no. Not at all. I'm used to it by now," I halfheartedly smiled.

***

Later that week, I was heading home from work and was thankful that I had once again made it through driving Jake's car without any damage. I was stopped at a red light a few blocks from my place when the whole car was jolted forward and a horrible crunching sound hit my ears.

Shit!

Shit, shit, shit.

I put the car in park, opened the door, and got out. The driver of the other vehicle did too. He looked sick to his stomach when he saw the kind of car he had just hit. I would have pegged him around eighteen, and I honestly felt really bad for him.

"I'm so sorry," he started. "Shit, I'm really sorry. Oh, man, I'm *so* sorry."

"Hey, it's okay," I reassured him, but I wasn't so sure it would be.

I met him at the back end of the car and assessed the damage with him. That was definitely not going to buff out. The entire back bumper was crunched in and not to mention all of the parking sensors, cameras, and lights that would have to be replaced.

"Shit, no," he began again, fisting his hair. "I can't afford this. Fixing something like that on a car like that is going to cost way more than I have."

"It's fine. Insurance will cover it," I said.

"I can't afford my deductible and my insurance will go up like crazy. I'm a broke college student. This is the last thing I need right now."

I could relate to where he was coming from. While I wasn't a broke college student, I was an almost broke college grad. I would be having a panic attack too if I had just hit this car, and I doubt this guy had a rich hockey player brother who could bail him out.

"Look, I get where you're coming from," I began. "Um, this isn't actually my car, though. I'm borrowing it from a friend, so I should probably call him and see if he can come down here."

The guy nodded and I went back to the car to grab my phone.

"Hey," Jake answered a moment later.

Even though I didn't cause the accident, I was terrified to call him. "Hi," I replied, my voice a little shaky.

He must have picked up on it. "What's wrong?" he asked.

"Um...I...um,"

"Olivia, what's wrong?" his voice was now panicked.

"Well, uh, I kind of got rear-ended and your car is pretty beat up and—"

"Right now? Where are you?"

"Yeah, um…I can send you a pin of where I am. I'm pretty close to my place."

"Are you okay? Do you need an ambulance or anything?"

"No, no. I just…I'm really sorry and—"

"I'll be right there." And he hung up on me.

Great, now *I* was the one crying.

~ 6 ~

Jake

Olivia had sent me a pin of where she was and I got there faster than I should have. I was kind of surprised at how quickly I did. I probably shouldn't have been driving that fast—it would have been quite ironic if I had gotten into a car accident while driving to one—but knowing Olivia had just been in an accident, I was panicking a bit. She said she was fine, but I had to see it for myself. I sprang from my car when I parked it in front of Olivia and rushed over to her and grabbed her in my arms and held her in front of me as if I was checking her for damages. Well, I *was* checking for damages.

"Are you okay?" I asked her again, not satisfied with the answer she had given me over the phone.

"No, your car is completely totalled. See I told you you shouldn't have let me borrow it. I know it wasn't my fault, but I still kind of—"

"Olivia!" I cut her off. "For fuck's sake. I don't give a shit about my car! I'm asking you if *you're* okay? Are you hurt?"

She stared blankly at me for a moment as if she couldn't quite comprehend what I was asking her. "Yeah. I'm fine," she finally replied.

"Are you sure? Did the airbags go off?"

"No," she shook her head.

"Okay," I sighed in relief and pulled her into my chest for a hug. When I released her, she still had that bewildered look plastered on her face.

Then she said, "Please be nice to the kid. He's sick over the fact that he wrecked an expensive car."

I smiled down at her, "Okay."

We walked over to the other driver. "Hey, man. I'm Jake," I held out my hand to the kid. That didn't seem to help with his panic attack though. He looked maybe eighteen or nineteen.

"Holy shit." Realization struck him as he stared at me. "I hit Jake Ellis's car." He threw his hands into his hair, fisting it at the sides and pacing.

I think the panicking was starting again.

"Hey, look man, it's okay," I replied.

"No it's not. I can't afford my insurance for this or fixing my own car. I have tuition payments I can barely afford and three jobs." He paused. "Sorry, that is *not* your problem." He managed to pull himself together. "I can give you my insurance information."

I looked at both cars and then back at the kid. "Look man, don't worry about it. I'll take care of this. I have a guy that does work for me. I'll get yours done too."

"What?" the kid replied in utter shock.

I glanced back at Olivia and her mouth was slightly agape too. I'm not going to lie; I liked the look of it—*but focus. Not the time.*

"You can't be serious?" the kid continued.

"I am. Just next time, pay attention more, okay?"

The kid nodded. "Yeah. For sure."

"Can you drive home? Are you okay?" I asked him.

"Yeah, I think so."

"Good. Give me your contact info and we'll be in touch."

The guy headed back to his car and a moment later came out and handed me a piece of paper with his name and number on it. I snapped a few pics of the damage on my phone and his driver's license and license plate.

"Okay," I took a breath when I was done. "We're all good here. Get home safely, okay?" I said to the kid. "I'll text you later this week with more info."

"Yeah. Thanks again Mr. Ellis. Wow, I really can't believe all of this."

I shot him a smile, "No worries. Just be careful."

He waved and got back into his car. I walked over to where Olivia was leaning against the driver's door of my damaged car, with her legs crossed at the ankles and arms across her chest.

"That was really nice of you," she started when I was standing in front of her.

I shrugged, "It was nothing."

"It was everything to him."

"Maybe."

"Seriously, Jake. Even for someone who makes as much as you do, I can't imagine anyone else would have just outright paid for all of this."

"Your brother would have."

"Yeah, but my brother's a goddamn saint." I smiled at that. Thatch really was. "This is going to cost you thousands."

I shrugged again. "Better me than the kid."

She looked down, "I'm really sorry again."

I moved in closer to her and took her hands in mine. "It wasn't your fault. Even if it was, I wouldn't care. I got that car for free anyway. For an endorsement deal I did last year."

Her expression shifted from guilt to anger pretty damn quickly. "You son of a bitch!" she slapped me across the chest.

I held my hands up in surrender, "Hey!" I paused and looked at her. "You sure you don't need to go to a hospital or something?"

"Like I can afford that," she rolled her eyes. I just glared at her. Obviously I would pay for it. "No, Jake. I'm fine. Not a scratch on me," she spun in place.

"Good. But let me know if you're not feeling well in the next couple of days."

"Okay," she sighed.

"Okay." I opened the car door for her. "Follow me to my place?"

"Yeah," she nodded.

When I pulled into my driveway, Olivia was right behind me. She parked the damaged car and got out. I was planning on getting Olivia over to my place in the next couple of days anyway to show her something.

She walked over to where I was standing and her gaze moved to something to my left. "Geeze, did you get a new car already?" she joked.

"Nope," I pulled the keys out of my pocket and held them up. "You did."

She stared at me and then shot her eyes to the car and back to me. "Jake!"

I jingled the keys in my fingers as if calling a dog to come, but she still didn't move. "Will you come here and take them?"

"No! You can't buy me a car!" she stomped her foot and crossed her arms. She was so fucking cute when she did that.

"Sure I can."

"No. You can't."

"Jesus, Olivia. Why do you have to be so goddamn stubborn?"

"What is my brother going to think when he sees me driving this thing? He's going to ask where it came from."

"How often do you actually see your brother?" I retorted. "As far as I know, you can probably get away with him not knowing for a few months and then when he does find out, you can say you bought it with your sweet promotion money you got because of how well you're doing at work because of me. Well, you can leave out the 'me' part, because he can't know that."

"Seriously Jake. I can't take this from you."

"Yes you can. I can't have my fake girlfriend driving around in whatever piece of shit you can afford. Look," I walked closer to her and took her hand and placed the keys in it. "I held back a lot buying this car. It's affordable and practical and something you could very plausibly have bought on your own." She looked at the keys in her hand and then over at the blue hatchback sitting on my driveway;

looking completely out of place. "Please. I can't return it, and there's no way in hell I would drive it, so you basically have to take it."

She slowly smiled at me and took small steps over to it. She unlocked it and got inside. Her lips were moving in a thinking motion as she gripped the steering wheel. "I guess…if you can't return it."

"I'm mean, I guess I could. But please don't make me walk into that dealership again."

She glanced over at me and smiled. "Okay. Thank you."

"You're welcome. It has a heated steering wheel and seats, so you'll love it in the winter."

"Cool," she nodded. She turned and a satisfied smirk grew on her face. "You care about me."

"What?" my head shot back. "Nope."

"Yes you do. You care about someone other than yourself." She got out of the car and stood in front of me.

"Not a chance. Just figured that if your brother ever does find out about this," I motioned between us, "this might make him hate me slightly less."

"No, you care. Jake Ellis cares about someone other than himself. This is amazing."

I flattened my lips. "So, should we go get it registered and make it officially yours?"

She threw her arms around me. I was *not* expecting that.

"Thank you, Jake. I know this probably didn't even put a dent in your credit card, but thanks."

My arm made its way around her back, "No problem, GT."

~ 7 ~

Olivia

I was surprised at work by Jake. I had told him that he could stop by sometime during the week and bring me coffee or something, but he didn't specify when he'd have time. So there I was, sitting at my desk, when a cup of coffee was suddenly placed before me. I looked up to see Jake smiling down at me.

"Hey," he greeted.

"Hi. Sorry, I'm just surprised to see you."

"You told me to come."

"I know. I just figured you'd text first."

"Where's the fun in that? I wanted to actually surprise my girlfriend. Or am I not your boyfriend anymore? How's Nathan?"

I glared at him. "Fine. I might see him again, I might not. Haven't decided yet."

"Lucky him…" he said with a passive indifference. "Anyway…"

I gave him a sideways smirk and took the coffee from my desk, "Thanks."

"So, can I take you to lunch?"

I shot my head back, "Wait, actually?"

"Sure, why not?"

"Because people will see," I pointed out.

"Isn't that the point?" I paused a moment and looked at him. "I highly doubt we'll run into your brother, if that's what you're worried about?"

"Yeah, but what if someone takes our picture or something and posts it somewhere and he sees it?"

"Okay…I did not think of that. But I'm sure it'll be fine," he assured me.

"Don't you have better things to do?"

"Nope, done for the day."

"Well—"

"Ellis!" we were interrupted by Henry coming over to my desk. "Good to see you again, man," he added, taking Jake's hand.

"Yeah, you too. I was just here to take Liv to lunch."

"Oh, yeah, you should go," Henry smiled at me.

"Um, okay. Let me just finish this email." I turned back to my computer and zoned out as the two of them talked for a moment.

"So, are we going to see you at the retreat next weekend?" asked Henry. That caught my attention and my head shot back toward them.

"Um, I'm not sure yet. I might be unavailable," Jake quickly responded. Wow, he was good at faking it.

"You sure?" replied Henry. "It's a great time. I'm sure Olivia already told you, but it's at this fancy resort in Aspen. Callaghan goes all out. Nothing you're not used to though, I'm guessing."

"Well, I can see. I might be able to swing it."

What was he saying? *Don't tell him that!* My eyes burned into him.

"Awesome. Well, I have to get back to work. Have a nice lunch, Olivia," and he headed off.

"What did you do that for?" I whisper yelled at Jake. "Now everyone is going to be expecting you at the retreat."

"Relax, I probably can't go anyway. Unless you really need me—"

"Don't," I cut him off. "I can't handle this right now."

"What? I just did exactly what your real boyfriend would have. Would I not try to go if I could?"

"Maybe. We will deal with this later. I'm starving." I got up from my desk and motioned for him to follow me.

Jake just watched me as I ate. It was weird. "What are you doing?" I finally asked him.

"Tell me more about this retreat."

"Seriously? You're not going. How would we even manage that? I don't think everyone will believe us if we're staying in two separate rooms."

"Well, is it going to affect your job somehow if I don't go?"

"No, why would it?"

"Your boss isn't going to use it against you?"

"How could he possibly use that against me? Yeah, I'm sure he'd love to spend an entire weekend living it up with his favourite hockey player, but he can't exactly fire me if you're busy."

"I know. But men like him seem to work in a different world," Jake added.

"Yeah, I know," I rolled my eyes.

"So, do you want me to try to go, or not?"

"I don't know. Wait. Would you actually be able to?"

"Yeah. I could probably swing it."

I stared at him. "You would actually do that for me?"

"Yes. Isn't that what we're doing here? I'm helping you with your career."

"Yeah, but…" I shrugged it off. "It's two weeks away. I'll just tell everyone you can't make it."

"Okay."

Later that week, I was getting into the elevator at work. I had just finished up sending some drafts over to Henry for another one of our biggest accounts and I was feeling pretty pleased with myself.

"Oh, hi Mr. Callaghan," I greeted him as he walked up beside me.

"Olivia, nice to see you," he smiled at me. I hopped into the elevator with him and Henry. They were going over some reports on Henry's tablet when he turned to me.

"So, is Ellis coming to the retreat?" Henry asked.

"Oh, no, he won't be able to make it."

"Hmm, that's a shame," Callaghan interjected. "Henry, I've been doing some reassessing, and I think it'd be best if you take the lead on the Kensington account. Can you do that?"

Wait, what? He said I would get it. "Sorry, I...I thought I was taking that one?" I found myself saying. Normally I would have just played dumb and not said a word, but they slipped from my lips before I could realize.

"Oh, no, sorry. I decided to give it to Henry and I have something else more worth your talent."

Prick. Total and complete asshole!

"Oh, Henry, sorry, I meant that Jake can't come for the whole retreat but he'll be there Friday afternoon to Sunday," I suddenly found myself saying.

"Awesome," he smiled.

"Is that so?" added Callaghan. "Henry, do you think you might need a partner on the Kensington account?"

"Um, sure."

"Olivia, you can partner with Henry."

The doors opened and Callaghan headed out to his office.

Maybe I was a pushover.

~ 8 ~

Jake

GT: *Ok, if you can come to the retreat, I would really appreciate it.*

Me: *Really?*

GT: *Yes.*

Me: *What changed your mind?*

GT: *My boss being an asshole.*

Me: *You know, GT, you really don't have to put up with that.*

GT: *Yes I do. For now at least.*

Me: *Alright fine. But if he's an asshole to you that weekend, I can't be held responsible for anything I might say or do.*

GT: *It's Thursday night to Sunday, but I already told them you'll only be there Friday afternoon to Sunday. I will send you all the details later. Thanks again, see you there.*

"Jesus, Ellis, who has you all distracted over there?"

"Huh?" I looked up from my phone at Thatch. Shit.

"Oh, no one."

"Really? Because whoever *she* is, and I'm quite positive it's a she, she's been blowing up your phone lately."

"It might be, but it's just a friend I'm helping with something."

"Alright, fine. If you don't want to tell me, that's cool. Say no more. You going to hit this thing or not?" he motioned to the tee box.

"Yeah, sorry." I slipped my phone back into my pocket and teed up. I hit the ball straight down the middle.

"Nice one," called Gabe.

"So, what's new, man? I've barely seen you lately," said Thatch as we were walking down the fairway.

"Not much, just been busy. Helping that friend, you know. What's new with you?"

"Greya wants a baby."

"Fuck, dude. No way. That's awesome!" I said clapping him on the back.

"Yeah. I just have to try to plan it so the baby's born during the off season."

"I don't think that's how that works."

"Yeah," added Gabe. "I'm convinced babies just happen."

"Well, maybe to you," mocked Thatch. "Do you even know how to use protection properly?" he continued mocking. "Do you need me to get a banana and show you?"

"Fuck you," retorted Gabe. "I know how to use it fine. We just have shitty luck is all... Or good luck, depending on how you look at it. The universe just decided we needed another kid before we did."

I knew both of Gabe's kids weren't exactly planned, but he was an amazing dad.

"Well, for future reference then..." continued Thatch.

Gabe shook his head. "Nope, we're done after this. I'm getting snipped."

"Oh, shit, dude," replied Thatch. "You're really sure two is enough?"

"Yup, we decided we're good."

"Well, maybe still wrap it up, just in case; with your guys' luck."

"Fuck you, again. I'm going to find my ball," and he started to walk off in the other direction.

"Just remember to pinch the tip," I called after him and was met with his middle finger in the air.

Turning back to Thatch, I restarted the him-having-a-baby conversation. "No, that's super cool, man. Congrats," I added.

"Well, she's not pregnant yet."

Thatch kicked both our asses at golf, and when I was heading home, it really hit me how much shit I would be in if he found out I was going away with his sister for the weekend. And I'm pretty sure she was right and we weren't going to get away with staying in separate rooms. Hopefully, there will be two beds at least, but if I remembered anything from Benny (I call Greya Benny because her last name is Bennett) rambling on and on about her books, there won't be.

The rest of my week went by as usual. I hadn't heard from Olivia so I was assuming everything was cool and we were still on for the retreat. I was packing my bag on Thursday evening when I got a call from her.

"Bad. Bad. Bad," she yelled into the phone.

"What is it?" I calmly replied.

"I just got to the hotel and my boss *very generously* upgraded us to a suite. With *one* bed!"

Called it.

"It'll be fine. Is there a couch?"

"Yeah."

"Okay, cool. I'll sleep there."

"Are you sure? It's pretty small, and you are definitely not. I don't think you'll fit. Maybe I can ask the front desk for a cot?"

It was cute how much she was freaking out right now. "Okay, look, take some deep breaths. We will figure it out when I get there. For now, just have a great first night."

"No, I can't do this. This was a bad idea. I knew it."

"You can do it, and everything will be fine. I promise," I reassured her. That girl was wound really tight. "Do they have a spa there? Get a massage or something and relax. I will see you tomorrow afternoon."

"Okay, I can probably do that."

"Alright. Anything else you need while you have me?"

"No. I think I'm good," she sighed. "Oh, wait. You golf right?"

"Yeah," I chuckled. "Actually, I was just golfing with your brother the other day."

"Good. Bring your clubs because I think a lot of the guys are golfing on Sunday and I'm sure my boss would love to do a round with you."

"Okay. Is that all now?"

"Yes."

"Okay then. Bye."

***

"Bro, you just killed me," yelled Thatch at the TV screen.

"Sorry, man. That's just the way it goes sometimes," I replied moving my controller.

"You guys both suck," added Gabe.

Guys' night at Thatch's was going well. Benny was upstairs with Gabe's wife, Stella, going over wedding stuff.

I was headed to the bathroom when I was cornered by Benny. "So, I know who you're hanging out with this weekend."

"Shhh," I whispered to her. "And, what are you talking about?"

"Oh please. You think I don't know about you two? I'm the one who has been keeping Owen out of your hair for a while."

"And I appreciate it, but seriously, we can't be talking about this."

"So, how's it going with her?"

"Fine. I'm helping her get ahead at work. That's all."

"Uh-huh," she crossed her arms.

"Don't 'uh-huh' me. You think I would actually be stupid enough to let this turn into anything more? I don't have a death wish." She just glared at me. "What? I'm her fake boyfriend for a while, that's all."

"Yeah, until you become her real one."

"That's not going to happen."

She scoffed, "Sure, it will. Look, Owen doesn't know and it's not like he'd give you the older brother talk in any nice sort of way anyway, so I'm going to just step in and give you the older sister talk. You do anything to hurt her, and I will tell Owen and send him after you."

"I'm not going to do anything."

"Good," she smiled.

"And I don't think you'd do that anyway. You know how pissed he's going to be if he finds out that you knew about all of this and were keeping it from him?"

"That won't be an issue," she stated. "I can handle him; I have boobs."

That *was* a really valid point.

"Well, anyway, none of that is going to happen, so can I go to the bathroom now?"

"Fine. Have fun this weekend," she smiled.

"Dude, you didn't get the beers," said Gabe when I got back from the bathroom.

"Oh, I forgot."

"I'll go get them," said Thatch, standing up. "I want to see how the wedding stuff is going with the girls anyway."

I looked at my phone, "Ah, you know what, I think I should actually head out."

"Really?" replied Gabe.

"Yeah, I have to be up early." I had to drive three hours to meet Olivia. I patted Gabe on the shoulder, "See ya, man."

"Yup, see ya."

When I got upstairs, I could hear Thatch arguing with Benny in the kitchen. "Seriously, Owen. You can't just let that go for one day? She was at your birthday and nothing happened. You agreed to have all of them in the wedding party. Did you think they just wouldn't interact somehow?"

"No. You can't just let her walk with Gabe instead?"

"That's weird. The maid of honour and best man walk in together. That's Stella and Gabe. You can't just switch it up because you don't want your sister walking with—"

"Hey guys," I interrupted.

"Hey. Dude, you don't care if you walk down the aisle with Stella, right?"

"Nope. I'll walk with whoever you tell me to."

"See," he turned back to Benny. "Ellis, doesn't care, so can't you just do this for me?"

"Can't *you* do *this* for me? For God's sake, Owen. If you really had such a problem with them being in the same proximity as one another, you wouldn't still be friends with him."

Ooo, called out.

Thatch glared at her and crossed his arms. "I don't appreciate you pointing out my irrationalities to me."

She smiled, but rolled her eyes. "Look, Olivia and Jake can walk together. What do you think is going to happen in the middle of our ceremony?"

"Nope, no way. There is no way those two are walking down the aisle together. End of story!"

"Ughhh," she called out. "Fine. We'll talk about this later."

"Alright, well, I was actually just going to head out," I added.

"Oh, really?" Thatch looked at me.

"Yeah, sorry. I have an early morning. I'll see you guys later though."

They were so cute together.

~ 9 ~

Olivia

Jake was going to be here in an hour. I was pacing back and forth in my massive suite of a hotel room, wondering what this weekend would be like. At the forefront of my mind was the fact that he would be staying in the same hotel room as me and we had definitely crossed the line of him just helping me out once for work. If my brother found out now, he'd be done for. But then again, we were already this far into it; there was no backing down now.

My head shot to the hotel room door when I heard the sound of it unlocking. In walked Jake. I froze. "Hi," I smiled, putting on a casual front. "How was the drive?"

"Good. Nothing exciting," he replied, walking in and putting his bag down. His very large bag. Why did he need that much stuff for two nights?

"Why is your bag so big?" I found myself asking.

"Huh? Oh…" He looked down at it and then moved to open it. "Because of this." He pulled something large out of the bag, followed by an air pump.

"Did you bring an air mattress?" I asked with a slight laugh.

"Yeah," he smiled.

"Wow, that was actually really thoughtful of you," I smiled again.

"Well, I am actually a thoughtful guy," he shot me a smile back, and proceeded to lay down the mattress and start inflating it. "See, GT. Now we don't have to worry about the bed situation at all."

I sat on the edge of the non-inflatable bed and waited until he was finished. "So, what are the plans for today?" he asked.

"Um, not much. This retreat is more just for fun and employee bonding and such. There aren't mandatory events or anything I have to partake in. So we can pretty much do what we want. There is a dinner tonight with everyone, but that's it."

"Okay, well, what do you feel like doing then?"

"I don't know. Can we just stay in the room all day?"

"That's probably not ideal. You do want your boss to actually see me, right?"

"I guess. You hungry? We could get lunch and then see what we feel like?"

"Sure," he smiled at me.

We grabbed a quick lunch at the café in the hotel and we were walking around the resort after when we bumped into Callaghan.

"Ellis," he called out. "Glad to see you made it."

"Yeah. Glad to be here," Jake wrapped an arm around me.

"So, you in for a round of golf on Sunday?"

"I sure am," he replied.

"Excellent. Tee time's at ten. Just a quick nine holes for our last day. We'll meet you on the course."

"I look forward to it," added Jake as he took my hand.

Callaghan headed past us, and we started walking. It took a moment for me to realize that we were still holding hands.

"So," I said, sighing and pulling my hand from his, "what do you feel like doing now?"

"Not sure. What do people do on corporate retreats?"

"I don't know. This is my first one," I shrugged.

"Well, we could head to the pool, or go for a hike or something. Or head into town."

"Um," I thought a moment. "It doesn't matter to me. I guess a hike sounds okay."

"A hike it is then. I'll find a good one when we're back at the room."

I changed into something more hike-appropriate when we got back to our room while Jake looked for one that wasn't too intense. He found one that should take us only a couple of hours round trip and wasn't too technical.

***

"You said this was a quick hike," I called out when we were hitting the three-hour mark.

"Well, it said it was only supposed to take a couple of hours to do the loop. That may be based on people walking faster, though," he called back.

"We're going to be late for dinner now."

"Relax," he said, brushing past me. "People will just think we got held up doing it," he winked back at me.

"Ugh. I don't need them thinking that!"

"They already do, sweetheart."

I let out a sigh. "Fine, but we better be getting close to the parking lot."

"I think we're almost back—I recognize that tree." I rolled my eyes and hoped he could feel my disdain from behind him. "See," he called with his arms outstretched about twenty minutes later when we came across the parking lot. "Nothing to worry about." He pulled his phone from his pocket. "And we still have plenty of time to do it before dinner."

***

Jake was super charming at dinner.

Too charming.

He was really working hard for me, or maybe it just all came naturally to him. Actually, yeah. I think he was just being his normal charming self. I don't know how that guy did it, but he had everyone in love with him by the end of the night. Even the women who knew nothing about hockey and hated the sport; they were now diehard fans.

He unlocked the door to our room and we headed inside. We both stopped in our tracks and stared at the collapsed pile of rubber on the floor.

"That was definitely inflated when we left, right?" asked Jake, looking at the pitiful air mattress.

"Yup."

"Well, I guess I'll blow it back up. Hopefully, it'll last the night."

I took a breath and let it out. "It's fine. You can just sleep with me." He looked back at me. "Not *with* me, but beside me, in that bed," I pointed.

"Relax, GT. I knew what you meant. I didn't think you wanted to have sex with me." I shifted slightly, feeling a bit uncomfortable. "You sure you're okay with this? I don't mind just sleeping on the couch."

"Yes, it's fine."

"Okay. Because your good girl reputation won't get tarnished from one night sleeping next to me," he winked.

I just crossed my arms and rolled my eyes. "I wasn't worried."

"Good," he smirked.

He changed into some joggers and a t-shirt and flopped onto the bed next to me.

"So, want to watch a movie or something?" I asked, knowing full well I was not ready to actually try to fall asleep next to that man.

"Sure."

We scrolled through the movies for a while until we picked one.

There we sat. Each of us on either side of the bed with a large amount of space between us. We were in identical positions; leaning against the headboard with legs outstretched, ankles crossed, and arms crossed over our chests.

"See, I knew you just picked this movie because of him," Jake pointed at the screen.

"Nah, she's not going to end up with him," I replied.

"What?"

"Yeah. He's blonde."

His head shot back, probably because he was becoming painfully aware of his own hair colour. It was nothing against him, but most movies and books tend to favour the dark-haired male lead. It was just facts. "What's that supposed to mean?" he asked, sounding slightly offended.

"No, there's going to be some other guy...oh, yep..." I watched as another character came into the scene, "right on cue. That's who she's going to end up with."

"What? She clearly hates that guy," he pointed out.

"Uh-huh. But he's tall, dark, and handsome and a bit dangerous. He has bad idea written all over him."

"Blonde guys can have bad idea written all over them too."

"Are you speaking from experience?"

"Maybe," he smirked at me. "You want to find out?"

"Nope."

"You have a thing for bad boys, don't you?"

I scoffed, "Yeah, sure. You figured me out."

"Alright, well, we'll just see how your little blonde theory pans out," he added. The movie went on and it was clear that I was right about the situation and it was clear that Jake was getting more and more annoyed about it. "Oh, no, your boyfriend is going to be crushed by that train."

"Will you stop it," I teased back and swatted my arm across the bed.

"What?! They didn't even kiss at the end. This movie sucked!" groaned Jake when it was finished. "So," he turned to me, "bedtime, I guess."

"Probably." I lifted my knees to my chest and pulled out the covers from under my butt and nestled myself underneath them. I shifted my shoulder when I snuggled down and reached a hand back to scratch it gently. He turned out the lights and suddenly the room was bathed in darkness.

I tried to fall asleep.

I tried so hard.

But I just couldn't. I kept shifting and scratching various places. I knew Jake was awake too. "Why is it that when you're trying to fall asleep you suddenly get itchy in random spots?" I asked, scratching my leg.

"I don't know," he chuckled. "You can't sleep either?"

"Nope," I replied, my back still turned to him. "I'm not sure if it entirely has to do with you, or if I just can't turn my brain off. It's probably a bit of both."

I tried to scratch my back again but couldn't reach and groaned slightly. "Here," he said, shifting closer to me and reaching the spot I was trying to get. When he was done I reached for my shoulder and massaged it slightly.

"You okay?" he asked.

"Yeah, my shoulder just hurts a bit. I guess I've been kind of tense lately. Maybe that's why I can't sleep."

"I thought you got a massage this morning?"

"I did, but I don't think one session can work everything out. That's why they want you to keep going back and spend tons of money. She didn't really use enough pressure."

"Why didn't you just ask her to use more pressure?" he asked in a condescending tone.

"I don't know. Because I always feel weird about that."

"Jesus Olivia. You need to start standing up for yourself."

"I can stand up for myself just fine. Besides, it was a scalp massage anyway, so she only did a bit of shoulders and neck."

"You got just your head rubbed?" he asked, as if that was the strangest thing in the world.

"A scalp massage. Yes."

"Why?"

"It's nice and relaxing. They use coconut oil and massage it into your scalp."

"You paid someone to rub your head?" I could hear the subtle snicker behind his voice.

"A *scalp* massage. It's probably called that for that very reason. What are you, fourteen?"

"Yes."

"Anyway. It's very nice. You should try it sometime."

"Oh, I know how good a head rub can be."

"Stop being weird," I shot back at him and could feel the smirk on his face even in the darkness. "It's relaxing and it stimulates and promotes growth." Okay, yeah, I heard what I said. Jake was now trying really hard not to burst out laughing. "Oh, shut up! Hair growth! You're hopeless."

He calmed himself and looked apologetically at me. "Here," he said, shuffling back over to me. "Can I?" he asked.

"Um, sure. I guess." He rubbed my shoulder and it was like his hands were magic. I'm sure a lot of women thought Jake Ellis had magic hands for one reason or another. "Thanks," I said after he was done.

"Better?"

"A bit. Good for now."

"I can do more if you want?"

"Um…this feels kind of like crossing that line we shouldn't."

"Yes. Right," he agreed.

"But you are really good at giving massages…"

"Lay on your stomach," he motioned to me. I did and shifted more to the middle of the bed. Then he was over me.

It hadn't occurred to me until right in that moment that if he was going to give me a back massage that he would be straddling my butt. At least he was on his knees, hovering over it. I couldn't feel anything but his strong hands on my back and it did feel amazing. He was still over my shirt, so it wasn't that sensual or anything. Just being a good fake boyfriend and helping a friend out.

I let my eyes close and I relaxed into his touch for a moment. "Ah," I suddenly jolted. "Not there."

"Hmm, someone's ticklish."

"No, I ju—Jake!" he tickled me again. "Seriously," I giggled. I shifted my hips and rolled onto my back under him. He stared down at me with a devilish glint in his eyes, and then he did it again. I couldn't control myself. I was giggling and convulsing beneath him. He finally did let up and rolled off of me. He rolled onto his side and sat up on his elbow, resting his head on his hand. He just smiled at me. "That wasn't nice," I scolded.

"It was kind of fun, though. I think it loosened you up a bit, too. You seem more relaxed."

"Uh-huh," I pressed my lips together and ran my tongue along the inside of my teeth.

We stayed there, facing each other for a moment, then he inched closer. My heart was pounding as we looked into each other's eyes and suddenly the darkness around us was becoming a mask to hide behind. "Do you ever think about that kiss?" I found myself asking.

"All the time," he answered, so confident in his response.

I took a breath and he was suddenly closer to me. "There you are, standing on that line again," I whispered.

"Yeah, but it's a fun place to be," he whispered back.

"We can't do this," I said.

"Can't and shouldn't are two different things, GT. We definitely *shouldn't*. But we also *definitely* could."

"My brother would kill you."

"Sounds like I'll die pretty happy," he smirked. "It might be worth it." Then he kissed me on the forehead and turned back to his side of the bed, shifting himself under the covers. I did the same, hoping that I would now finally get some sleep, although I will never get the image of Jake Ellis straddling me while I was on my back out of my head now.

~ 10 ~

Jake

Mmmm. I love waking up next to a woman. I reached a hand down and felt her soft, sexy leg draped over me. I ran my hand up and down the smooth skin for a moment and then I heard her moan,

"Jake."

Yeah, baby. Say my name. She moaned again and pressed her butt into my side. I kept running my hand up her thigh. *Ohhh*—my eyes shot open—*livia!* My hand froze. I was inches away from having my hand up Thatch's sister's cute little flowered pajama shorts. I removed my hand and glanced over at her. She was lying on her back, sideways on the bed, with one leg draped over my hips. She was still sound asleep—thank God! I slowly shifted myself out from under her and she just rolled over and gave a little sleepy moan and snuggled right back in.

That was too close.

I had to get out of there. I quickly grabbed some other clothes and headed into the bathroom to change. Then I was out the door trying to erase the sound of her moaning my name from my memory.

When I got back to the room a couple of hours later, she was sitting on the bed doing something on her laptop. "Hi," she said when I walked in. "Where did you go?"

"I went for a run."

She did a once-over of me. "You should go shower. You're all…sweaty," she said in a way like it bothered her. Not in a normal, because you're gross way, but in a, it's getting me all hot and bothered way.

"Yeah, that tends to happen when I workout," I replied. We locked eyes for a moment. "Okay, I'll go shower then." And I headed into the bathroom.

Shit! I didn't bring my clothes with me. I wrapped a towel around my waist and headed into the bedroom after my shower. Her eyes followed me the whole way to my suitcase and back to the bathroom. When I emerged again, fully clothed, I sat on the edge of the bed at her feet. "So, want to get some brunch?"

"Sure," she smiled and closed her laptop.

"Did you sleep well?" I asked when we were seated at a table, and she was enjoying some pancakes.

"Hmm?" she looked up from her plate. "Uh, yup. Great."

"Good."

"Did you?" she asked.

"Yup," I nodded. "Great also."

"Good," she gave a quick smile.

"So, what should we do today?" I asked.

She shrugged. "I don't know. There's another group dinner tonight, but the rest of the day is free for us to do whatever we want. Oh, I do have a facial booked later with Keira, though."

"That sounds nice. I might go to the driving range then. Get in some swings before my game with your boss tomorrow."

"That sounds fun," she smiled.

"Want to go with me?"

"Uh…probably not. I don't golf."

"What?" I asked slightly shocked. "You've never been golfing? Not even with your brother, or dad?"

She shook her head in response. "It never really interested me."

"Well," I began again. "Do you want to try it now? What time is your facial? We can go after."

She thought for a moment. "Sure, I guess."

***

Well, I never thought someone could miss that many balls before. I don't think Olivia hit a single one.

"You need to keep your head down and your eye on the ball," I tried to instruct, standing behind her. "You keep looking up when you're swinging the club."

"Ugh," she let out an exasperated groan. "See, this is why I don't golf. I'm not good at swinging and hitting things. I don't have good eye-hand coordination."

"Well, duh. It's hand-eye for one thing. But once you get it, it'll be easy. Can I help you more now?" She had been resisting me helping her more than just a few pointers here and there. She practically leapt into the air when I touched her hips to turn her slightly into a better position.

"Fine," she groaned again.

"Okay," I said, coming up behind her and reaching around to take the club in my hands. I placed it back in hers and adjusted her grip and position. I could feel her back pressing into my chest and I was doing everything in my power to not grind up against her ass. I leaned down more and talked right next to her ear and caught a whiff of her shampoo or something because it took me a moment to regain my train of thought. "Now line it up and don't take your eye off the ball." I playfully swayed back and forth with her while moving the club and lining up the shot. Our hips rocked side to side in sync with one another and when she was ready, we drew back and followed through with the swing. She finally got that ball off the tee, and it actually went decently far.

"I did it!" she exclaimed, turning in my arms.

"See, I told you you could," I smiled down at her. "Want to try again?"

She nodded and moved away from me to get another ball. She managed to hit a few more after that, and she was beginning to love it.

"Hey, nice shot," called Henry from beside me.

"Thanks," I replied after I had sent the ball a good two-hundred and fifty yards.

Henry teed up beside me and his wife, who we had met last night at dinner, went beside Olivia.

"Are we going to see you two at dinner tonight?" asked Henry.

"I think so," I replied, looking at Olivia for confirmation.

"Yeah, we'll be there," she smiled.

We stayed at the driving range a bit longer and chatted more with Henry and his wife. They were nice and I was glad that Olivia had someone at her company that truly recognized her talent and wasn't just favouring her because of me. I didn't know it for sure, but any interaction I had with the man, it seemed that her boss would give her the obligatory compliment she deserved in front of her 'boyfriend', but then he would just talk to me the entire time. I hated guys like that. She was still basically invisible to him, but I could never tell her that. She was so happy thinking she was finally getting somewhere in her career.

Olivia looked banging in her cocktail dress for dinner. God, I wish I were her real boyfriend and then I could have ripped it off of her and made us late for dinner. When we arrived at the restaurant, her boss seated us right next to him, obviously.

"Ah, Olivia, take a seat here. And Ellis, you can have this one," he smiled at me; his not-so-perfect, crooked teeth grin. Yeah, I definitely saw some dental work needing to be done. I smiled back anyway and sat in the chair.

"You're going to have to tell Olivia she's allowed to actually relax on this retreat, Carter. Every chance she gets, I find her still working," I joked.

"Ah, that's our little Olivia. Like the Energizer bunny, always going. That's why I hired her."

Bullshit. You didn't hire her and you had no idea who she was until a few weeks ago. And she's not a child. 'Little Olivia'? What the fuck? "Well, I suppose her work ethic is one of the things I love about her," I said back, making sure to emphasize that fact that she was a hard worker and he was absolutely in the wrong for seeing her any other way.

"Mr. Callaghan," started Olivia. "When you get a minute tonight, I would like to quickly discuss some changed for the Greyson account."

He waved her off and didn't even look at her. "Of course, when I get the chance. Or just run them by Henry. I'm sure he'll do what's best."

He was seriously going to be testing my reserve tonight to not throttle him.

When dinner was done, we were all invited to the speakeasy-style cocktail bar in the hotel for some drinks. I was standing at the bar, ordering one, when Callaghan walked over. He stood next to me and I glared down at him; all five-foot-nothing of him.

"Wonderful dinner tonight, wouldn't you say?" he began. "I always think the steak here is the best you can find."

"It was great," I agreed. I will give him that. The steak was probably one of the better ones I had ever had. The bartender handed over my drink. "Well, Carter," I clapped him on the shoulder, "I should be getting back to

Olivia, and then I think we'll head in after this drink. See you tomorrow for that golf game."

"Ah, yes. Bring your A-game."

"I always do." *Prick.*

I found Olivia sitting on one of the couches talking to Keira and Henry and his wife. I sat myself next to her and put my arm around her shoulder as if it was the most natural thing in the world and a daily occurrence for us. She shifted into me slightly and my heart jumped. I sipped my drink as I listened to her and her co-workers talk about their projects and bounce ideas off of one another. I might be biased, but everything that came out of Olivia's mouth was the greatest idea I had ever heard. Her balding boss was seriously missing out. When we had all finished our last drinks, we said goodnight to everyone and headed back to our room.

"Tonight was fun," started Olivia.

"Yeah. Keira and Henry are really nice. I'm glad you have a couple of good co-workers." She just glanced over at me and smiled as her hand brushed mine as we were walking, sending another jolt to places all over my body.

We were almost back at our bungalow suite when it started to rain. We booked it for the door but it was no use; we were soaked. Olivia burst through the door of our room and headed straight for the bathroom. She emerged momentarily and tossed me a towel.

"Well, that was unexpected," she said while drying her hair.

"Yeah," I replied, secretly hoping my golf game with her boss would be rained out tomorrow. She headed over to her suitcase and pulled out some new clothes then headed back to the bathroom to change.

I changed too and a moment later I heard her calling out to me, "Hey, can you boil some water? I'm going to make a tea."

"Yeah, sure," I called back and flipped on the kettle. A minute later, it was boiling, but Olivia was still in the bathroom. "What kind do you want?" I asked her from the other side of the door.

"Oh, uh, just the green that's there. Thanks."

I made her tea, and a moment later she appeared in the room, now in sweats and a hoodie. I went to hand her the tea, but she wasn't paying attention and bumped into me, causing the scalding liquid to spill all over the front of her chest and stomach.

"Shit," I called out and instinctively grabbed her hoodie and pulled it off her, then grabbed hold of her and pushed her into the bathroom. She may have been protesting and asking what I was doing, but I didn't care. I had one objective in that moment. I shoved her into the shower and positioned the spray of cold water directly on her stomach.

"Ahh!" she called out when the cool water hit her.

"Are you okay?" I asked. "I'm so sorry. The burn doesn't look too bad."

"Yeah, I'm fine," she replied. "How long am I going to stay here like this?"

"I think burn protocol is you stay under the water for about twenty minutes."

"Twenty minutes, huh? You going to stay here with me the whole time?"

I looked down at her dripping wet body and perfect chest now speckled with goosebumps, and the lacy pink bra she had on. "I'm thinking about it."

"I'm starting to get cold," she shivered.

"Sorry, but it hasn't been twenty minutes."

She smiled up at me, "So, is this the time I tell you that you really didn't get me with the tea."

"What?"

"Yeah, my hoodie was thick enough it didn't really hit me, plus you ripped it off of me impressively fast." She gave her head a slight shake, "No burn."

"You're such a brat," I smiled, moving closer to her and placing the shower head back into its holder and pointing it away from us.

"So…can you turn the heat up now? I'm still freezing."

"Uh-huh," I replied, inching closer to her and dragging a hand up her side all the way to her cheek.

"I meant the shower."

"I know what you meant." I stared into her eyes for what felt like an eternity, listening to the devil on my one shoulder and the angel on the other; trying to make my decision about what I should do next. She wasn't moving though either. Wasn't pushing me away. Wasn't getting out of the shower. She just stared back, us intimately close to one another. "You have no idea how long I've wanted to kiss these lips again," I ran a thumb over them gently. "And properly this time."

She let out a breathy whisper, "Fuck, me."

"Oh, I want to. And someone who looks like you shouldn't be allowed to say those words without a warning attached to them."

"We should stop before we do something we can't come back from."

Fuck it. I didn't care that she was Thatch's little sister. I cared about her and I just wanted her. "Jesus, GT. I'm so far gone already, you have no idea. There's no coming back from this." I pushed her against the shower wall and my lips were on hers before she could register what was happening. I did turn the water temperature up too with my other hand, but most of the heat in that shower was coming from us. Our kiss was hard and desperate and she returned everything I was giving her. I reached down and pulled her legs up around my waist and kissed her even harder, devouring every movement of her lips, claiming her, and swallowing any sound that came from them. I moved to her neck and I could hear her moaning with pleasure as I peppered it with more searing kisses. Then I reared my head back and looked at her. We had definitely crossed that line, but still hadn't gone so far over it that we couldn't even see a glimpse of it anymore.

"We should stop," she finally managed to get out.

"I don't want to."

"But we should. I don't think this is a good idea."

"It's an excellent idea."

She gave me a smile and I lowered her back to standing on the shower floor. She turned off the water and walked out.

I ran a hand through my wet hair. *Fuck.* That was definitely worth the ass-kicking I'll get from her brother later, but now what?

When I had dried myself off from the shower I decided to take after being left alone in it, I headed back into the room to find Olivia in her pajamas and on her phone in bed. The night was going to be awkward, to say the least.

"I can sleep on the couch tonight if you want?" I offered. I didn't really know what to say after having possibly the best make-out session of my life and then being left by the girl.

"No, it's fine. You can still sleep here. We just...we just can't repeat what just happened. Or anything more."

"Okay..." I replied, walking over to my side of the bed and getting in. "Why not?"

She turned to face me. "You know why not. We're just pretending. This isn't real."

"Felt pretty real to me," I looked at her.

"It doesn't matter." She turned back over and turned out her light and snuggled in to go to sleep.

And that was that.

End of conversation.

When I awoke the next morning, Olivia had managed to move herself right next to me again in her sleep and was still in that blissful state between sleep and awake I longed to stay in forever. I turned over and spooned her. I wasn't in the habit of spooning women in my bed, but I would make an exception for her; I would make all the exceptions for Olivia. If I couldn't have her when we were out of this little bubble, I was going to keep pretending right here for as long as she would let me. She snuggled back into me more and I laid there for a few minutes, taking in the feeling of her in my arms and her quiet breathing until she began to wake up. She turned to look at me and seemed slightly sorry that she had moved over to me while she was sleeping, but she didn't say anything about it. She just scooted away and grabbed her phone from the nightstand to check the time.

"Should we go get breakfast before your golf game?" she asked.

"Uh, yeah," I replied, looking at my own phone and seeing that it was eight-thirty.

We got dressed in silence, and then headed to the restaurant for the breakfast buffet.

***

Fuckity, fuck, fuck, fuck!

Golf did not go well.

Well, no, the golf did go well. I let her boss beat me by only a couple of points, but I heard him talking to one of the other guys after that he didn't think Olivia had it in the company and he was just using her to get to me. I knew it! Apparently, I would be a great *asset* to have as a way to entice companies to sign with them. You know, if he could convince them they could have an NHL star backing their company. I would be a great marketing resource. Fucking bastard!

I found Olivia on one of the hotel patios just looking at her phone with some sort of girl frappuccino thing in her hand. "Hey," she said when she noticed me standing before her. She smiled, "How did it go?"

"Good. I let your boss beat me." She shifted her weight and pursed her lips at me. "What? He wouldn't have otherwise." I sat on the chair next to her. "How was your pedicure?"

"Good," she smiled, holding out her foot and pointing her toes for me to see.

"Red. Sexy," I smiled. I had to tell her. There was no way I couldn't. "So, look…" I took my baseball hat off and held it in my hands, bending the brim between them. "I have to tell you something."

Her face turned skeptical. "What?" she asked.

I took a deep breath and blew it out. Then I looked around. *Maybe not here, maybe we should go somewhere more private.* "Come with me." I took her hand and led her inside and down an empty hallway. "Ah, fuck, GT. Look…I overheard your boss talking to one of your co-workers after the game and I guess he doesn't actually think you have what it takes for his company. He's just hoping that by keeping you around he can get to me and I'll help with promotion and stuff for his clients." Fuck; the look on her face. I inched closer to her. "You okay?" I leaned down and tried to look at her. I moved in even closer and cupped her face in my hands and pulled it toward me. "Hey, he's a complete jackass and if you want, I'll go kick his ass right now?" She smiled slightly, but I could see the tears coming. "Liv, come on. You don't need this job or his seal of approval. You're better than this."

"No, Jake," she pushed me off her. "Why did you tell me all of this?"

My head shot back. *What?* "Jesus, Olivia. Because I care about you." I moved in closer and pushed her against the wall. My hands cupped her cheeks again. "You shouldn't be working for an asshole like that. He's just buttering you up to get to me. This can't possibly be what you want?"

"I don't have a choice," she shot back and pushed me off of her again. Then she turned to head out of the hotel entrance and headed to her car. I jogged after her and matched her pace when I caught up.

"Quit your job, Olivia! It's not worth it."

"I can't do that, Jake!" She swiveled in place and stared up at me, anger beaming in her eyes. "I don't have the luxury of getting to do what I love and be paid millions of dollars to do it. I have rent and bills and food to pay for. This is the only place that hired me, and I honestly have no idea why now. But the point is that if you shattered your leg tomorrow and could never play hockey again, you'd still be set for life. I don't have that. So if that means being a pushover for my asshole boss, then so be it."

"Jesus, Olivia. Why do you like fighting with me so much? You know I'm the only person you can stand up to, right?"

"What? What does that have to do with anything?"

"Stand up to your fucking boss! Just imagine he's me when you're telling him off."

"I can't!"

I sighed. "Fine. I guess you're an adult and can make your own decisions." I ran a hand through my hair. "I have to get going now, too, but I guess if you still need me to play boyfriend, let me know." Then I headed for my car and watched as she got into hers and headed home.

~ 11 ~

Olivia

By the end of the week, I had had it. After what Jake had told me, that was all I could think about. It consumed my thoughts at work. I thought that maybe Jake was just the key I needed to get noticed, and everything else was me. That Jake had just made my boss notice my talents, but I was wrong. Completely and utterly wrong. Callaghan didn't care about me at all. All he wanted was an NHL superstar for promotional material. How could I be so stupid? Jake was right. I didn't need this job. Well, I did. I really did because I couldn't pay rent otherwise, but that was beside the point and I would figure it out later. Owen would gladly pay my rent for me if I asked.

What was more confusing was the way Jake acted. He cared about me. He said it himself and I was starting to care about him too—maybe more than just care about him. I pretended to be asleep the first morning of the retreat when he was caressing my leg but he must have realized what he was doing and didn't want to cross that line, but I felt it. I was starting to feel all of it; for him. Then the next night when he thought he had burned me and that kiss in the shower was all I could think about, when it was just the two of us in that hotel room and him holding me tight in bed the next morning.

I was sitting in a meeting with Callaghan, Henry, Brian, and Keira when it all hit me. Every word coming out of that smug bastard's mouth hit like a punch to the gut. He was never going to see me as more than Jake Ellis's girlfriend.

"You good with that, Olivia?"

I snapped back to it and looked up to see Callaghan staring at me. "What?"

"Are you okay with working with Brian on the Hathaway account?"

"You know what? No," I stood up, summoning my inner confidence. I felt like a five-year-old in a Superman shirt; I could do anything. "Actually, I'm not cool with it and I'm not cool with any of it. I know that you're just using me to get to Jake. I know that you don't think I actually benefit this company in any other way than being Jake Ellis's girlfriend. I want to go somewhere where I'm actually recognized for *my* talent, and I'm good enough. Because I *am* talented, damn it! I'm great at what I do, and all those pitches you loved months ago that came from Brian, were actually mine. So suck it. I quit!"

They all stared at me, and I could see the glimmer of a smile creeping onto Henry's face.

"Yes, girl!" called Keira.

"You can't quit!" Callaghan stood from his chair.

"Oh yes I can! Just watch me."

***

An hour later, I was at Jake's doorstep. I had gathered my things right after I had finally told Callaghan off and just walked right out of there. There was no way I was sticking around until the end of the day and for some reason I didn't go home like a normal person would, I headed straight for Jake's place. I was hoping he was home and I was only now wondering why I hadn't texted him that

I wanted to come over, but I also kind of wanted to surprise him. I rang his doorbell, but there was no answer. I tried again a couple of times. Then I finally decided to text him.

Me: *Are you home right now?*

Jake: *Yes. Why?*

Me: *I'm at your door.*

Jake: *That's you? Sorry, I'm in the hot tub.*

Me: *It's fine, I can let myself in.*

I put my phone back in my pocket and used the code Jake had given me to let myself in.

"Hey," I called out. "Where are you?"

"Out here," I could hear Jake's faint voice calling back.

I finally found him on his deck in the hot tub. I stepped through the door and was about to walk over to him when he held a hand up and halted me.

"I should probably tell you that I'm naked in here."

I rolled my eyes. "Of course you are. Why?"

"It's *my* house."

"Don't you have one of those doorbell cameras? You could have found out it was me."

"I didn't want to be bothered," he put his head back and rested it on the side of the tub.

"Whatever. I have something to tell you." He looked up and met my eyes with his, then a giant grin crept onto my face; high off the feeling of quitting.

"What is it?" he asked.

"I quit my job."

"What?!" he jerked forward slightly as if he was going to stand, but then remembered he would have flashed me if he did.

"Yeah, I actually did it. Just this afternoon. Actually, about an hour and a half ago."

"Fuck yeah!" He glanced over at the towel next to the hot tub. "Can you turn around?"

"Oh, yeah," I said turning. What I did not expect was the reflection that could be clearly seen in his windows. *Oh my!*

"Okay, you can turn around now," he said, and I turned to find him standing there dripping wet with a towel around his waist. I think I preferred him staying in the hot tub—well, maybe.

He walked over to me and motioned me inside. "Wait here," he said, then headed upstairs. He returned a few minutes later fully clothed. He was casual, just jeans and a t-shirt, but he looked good. He annoyingly always looked good. He smiled when he caught my gaze and ran toward me and picked me up and spun me around. "I'm so proud of you," he added when he placed me back on the ground.

"I'm proud of me too. I'm also completely scared of what I will do now, but it'll be okay. I'll manage."

"Yeah you will. And if you need anything, let me know. You want me to pay a year's worth of rent for you? Done. You want food deliveries daily? That's done too."

"Thanks," I chuckled. "And I'm sorry about the last day of the retreat. I know you were just trying to help and I shouldn't have yelled at you. So…look. I guess we don't need to do this fake dating thing anymore. And since we only made it a little over a month into the thing, we can call it off. You were a perfectly loyal boyfriend, as far as I know, so feel free to go sleep with whoever you want now. We don't need to go on that date. We can just call it even."

"Are you kidding me?!" he called out. "You just made me help you with your stupid work life and not hook up with anyone for the last *six weeks*—yeah, I'm counting—to prove to you that I'm not just some sort of pig that sleeps with whatever pretty thing bats her eyelashes at me, and now you're backing out? Nuh-uh. No. We're going on that date, right now," he added, grabbing my hand and leading me toward the garage. "And I will be kissing you goodnight after and there will be some boob or butt fondling—I haven't decided which yet. I think I made it pretty obvious in that shower that you're the only one I want."

I took his hand and let him lead me, then I pulled him back as the reality of the evening ahead struck me, "Look, I think I should maybe tell you something." He turned back to look at me. "I've…uh…I've never actually slept with a guy before."

"What?!" He was completely taken aback. "You've seen you, right?" I just shrugged. "Sorry, I'm just trying to wrap my head around the fact that you've never had sex before. You know you're a smoke show." He took a slight step back and looked me up and down. "You? The girl who drunkenly made out with me years ago? And I'm not gonna lie, I think I remember some grazing of something—now I'm really regretting saying I was going to fondle your boobs later."

I let out a small laugh. "You wouldn't be the first guy, don't worry. I've just never gone all the way."

"But why?"

I shrugged. "I don't know. It's not like I never had the chance. I dated and had boyfriends, but most guys when they find out who my brother is, they either only want to be with me for the bragging rights and they completely forget I exist and just want to get close to him. Or it scares them off for some reason, so it never really felt right."

"Well, as someone who has been on the receiving end of your brother's punches, I can see where they're coming from."

"You were kind of right that night in the bar bathroom. Guys seem to only care about who my brother is. I guess people have been using me to get to someone else my whole life. Honestly, that night three years ago, I probably would have slept with you just to get it over with. That's why I kissed you. I had just broken up with my boyfriend earlier that week and I needed some cheering up, so Owen invited me to that party. When I saw you there, I just wanted to do something reckless and impulsive for once in my life. I knew you and your reputation, so I figured you were my best bet."

"Well, you didn't figure wrong, I mean… But you shouldn't just sleep with someone to get it over with. It should be someone you care about and feel comfortable with. Otherwise, it's going to suck and will probably turn you off of it forever. Okay, not forever, but you know what I mean."

"Look, I get it if you don't want to deal with all of this or actually date me now."

"What? Why the fuck would I care? Actually, it's pretty hot knowing that you'll be only mine. But I'm definitely not going to fuck your brains out after this date like I was originally planning on doing."

I chuckled, "Are you sure you want to do this then? To actually date me? And what about my brother?"

He shrugged. "I can deal with Thatch. Better to ask forgiveness than permission, right? We'll probably have it out and he'll punch me again, but then he'll be cool."

"Okay," I smiled. "If you're sure about it?"

"GT, I've never been more sure of anything in my entire life. I've liked you since the moment I met you. Then I found out that you were Thatch's little sister, and it didn't matter. You were off-limits so I made it my mission to forget about you. But then you just had to kiss me at that damn party and for the last three years, I couldn't get you out of my head."

I looked at him for a moment, then just like that night three years ago, I bridged the gap between us and kissed him. It was a quick, soft kiss. I pulled back and smiled at him.

"I can't believe I let a virgin push me around for the last month," he joked with a wry smile. I laughed while he reached his hand behind my head and grabbed a fistful of my hair and pulled me back to him. He locked our lips and pulled me in closer, merging our bodies and releasing the full force of his desire on me. He slowly walked me backward to the couch and when the back of my legs hit it, he turned and lifted me on top of him as he sat down. We stayed there for I don't know how long; with me straddling his lap and him devouring me with kisses. Eventually, he laid me down and nestled himself between my legs, but we didn't break the contact of our lips.

"Hey," I managed to break our contact.

"Mmhhm?" he responded while nestled in my neck, planting kisses all over it.

"Do you mind if we just stay in tonight? I mean, I guess if you really want to take me out you can, but I think I'd rather just have a night in."

He looked up, "Oh, no. We're definitely staying in now. I can't do this to you at a restaurant." I smiled. "Want to order something in? What are you feeling?"

"Umm…pasta."

"Pasta it is then."

After dinner, I was sitting on Jake's kitchen counter while he put our dishes in the dishwasher. "So," I began. "What are we going to do about my brother?"

He closed the dishwasher and walked over to me. "I think we should forget about him for a while, and we'll tell him when it feels right. We just started this thing, so let's just be us and see where it goes for a bit."

"Sounds good. Greya's going to figure it out right away, though. You know that?"

"Yeah. Well, she can keep a secret. She has so far."

"What about the wedding in a few weeks?" I added.

"I think it'll be fine. We'll keep our distance and act like everything is the same as usual."

"Okay."

"Look, I know you're nervous about all of this, but I honestly think it'll be fine. Your brother isn't going to suddenly disown you or anything," he touched a hand to my cheek.

"I know," I leaned into it, then wrapped my arms around his neck.

"Even if he did…it might be worth it," he winked.

"So how are things with the hockey player?" asked Keira when she was at my place for girls' night the next week.

"Oh, um. Good. We actually called the whole thing off because I quit my job."

"So, you're not still seeing him?"

"Well…"

"Nice," she smiled. "See, you do have it in you; to not be a good girl all the time. Maybe you're growing up. I'm so proud."

"Thanks. Anyway, it's good. I really like being with him and he's amazing."

"And hot."

"Yes, that too. So hot! Honestly I don't know how I handle myself around him."

She chuckled, "So, how did your brother take it?"

"Umm," I shoved a few chips in my mouth. "We haven't told him yet."

"Okaayy. You're his little secret; I like it. Wow, you're learning to be a rebel pretty quickly being around him."

"Oh please. I'm still me. We just decided that it's best to see where this goes before we risk his life by telling Owen. What if it doesn't work out? Then he might be in even more shit for not only dating, but breaking up with his best friend's little sister."

"I guess I can see that. Do you think it's going somewhere?"

"I don't know. I'm crazy about him and I never expected to be." I changed the subject, though. "So, how's work without me?"

"Same as usual. I'm thinking I might follow suit and quit though. You really inspired me. Henry is even talking about possibly starting his own firm and if he does, he would want us to work for him."

"What, really?"

"Yeah. Crazy, right?"

***

A few days later, I was on the hunt for a new job. Even with this possible Henry offer, I had no idea how long it would take, and I needed stable employment until then. I had told Greya what had happened and she wasn't at all surprised. She agreed to help keep our secret until we were ready to tell. Then I got a phone call from my brother.

"Hey," I answered.

"Hey, Liv. Greya told me you quit your job. Are you okay?"

"Oh, yeah. I'm fine."

"What happened?"

"My boss is a total asshole, you know that, and it turns out that he was just praising me for my work because…uh…he found out that you're my brother and he was trying to get to you I guess. I guess he hoped that he might be able to use you in some marketing campaign. You know, hockey players are a great marketing asset. Anyway, I'm all good and I'm actually really glad to be rid of that job. I want to be somewhere where they appreciate and recognize me for my talent, not my name."

"Yeah, for sure. Well, I'm really glad you stood up for yourself and quit. That's awesome. You have trouble with that sometimes, and I'm glad you're happy and you didn't just stick it out for the paycheck. Are you sure you're good, though? Do you need rent money or anything?"

"No, Owen, I'm fine," I grumbled slightly.

"Are you sure?"

"Yes. You'll be the first person I call if I need money."

"Okay. I have to go now, but I guess I'll see you in a couple of weeks."

"Yup, bye."

I hung up the phone. That conversation would have been a lot less anxiety inducing if I hadn't been sitting on Jake's couch.

~ 12 ~

Jake

Alright, I was definitely going to be in a lot of shit for this later, but I didn't care. The last week with Olivia was probably the best week of my life, and I wasn't even having sex—which was new for me.

"So, can we please re-discuss this whole bachelor party thing?" I asked Thatch after the gym. "We can't not throw you one."

He just shrugged, "I'm really not the bachelor party type."

"Well, it doesn't have to be wild, but a night with your bros doesn't sound that bad."

"How would it be different than any other night I hang out with you guys?"

"I don't know. It'll be more bachelor party themed—" He opened his mouth to speak but I cut him off, "without strippers."

"Maybe," was all I got out of him.

"Come on. Isn't Benny doing a bachelorette party? Some spa day or something...you mentioned." Shit, I wasn't actually sure if it was him that mentioned it to me, or if it was Olivia, but hopefully I could gaslight him into thinking he did tell me.

"Yeah, she is. But that's also hardly a bachelorette party. She's just getting together with Stella and my sister, I think. Maybe Gabe's sister too."

"Still sounds nice. We can spa it up if that's what you want too?" I mocked with a shoulder nudge.

"Thanks, but I'm good." He sighed, "Okay, I guess something casual and low-key is fine. But just you and Gabe. And maybe a couple of the guys on the team—shit, we're going to have to invite the whole team aren't we?"

"Nah," I shook my head. "We can keep it small. I'll talk to Gabe and we'll come up with something great. Something that screams, Thatcher's getting married."

"I don't want any screaming."

"Something that speaks in a very normal tone, Thatcher's getting married."

"Sounds great," he smiled. "God damn it, why are my knees so sore?"

"Well, maybe you shouldn't have spent all day yesterday crawling through one of those indoor jungle gyms with Elsie."

"Maybe."

"You're going to wear yourself out before you have kids," I joked.

"Well, I guess you'll just have to chase after my kids for me," he retorted.

"Not a chance. You will never see me crawling around one of those jungle gyms."

"You say that now…"

"Nope," I shook my head.

We managed to throw together a pretty chill night for Thatch's bachelor party. True to my word, I stuck to nothing over-the-top, no strippers, no limos, no fun—I mean no excessive alcohol. It was great, though. We started with whiskey tasting at this brewery and then headed to this upscale steakhouse—that does *not* look like my house—for a privately booked out event. The whole place was ours and we spent all night there, drinking and eating.

"Alright, Ellis, this is a pretty great bachelor party. Thanks for convincing me," slurred Thatch, thumping down beside me after dinner.

"No problem. You deserve it and we're all thrilled you found someone like Benny."

"Thanks. She really is the best and I can't believe I managed to convince her to marry me."

"Hey, don't sell yourself short. You're the best guy I know and the only guy for her. You two were meant for each other."

"Thanks. This is weird, you being all sentimental and lovey and crap. What's with you?"

I shrugged, "Nothing. I can't be happy that my best friend is getting married to the love of his life?"

"Oh, you can. It's just weird hearing you say the word love so many times," he mocked with a sip of his drink.

"Well, maybe things are changing."

His eyes narrowed on me and his lips quirked at one side, "Does this have to do with that girl? The secret one you won't tell anyone about?"

"Maybe. But I'm not talking about it tonight. This is your night. We are celebrating you and Benny and your end to bachelorhood," I held up my glass to his and we toasted.

"Hey guys," said Gabe, sitting beside us. "Good call on this place Ellis. This is probably one of the better bachelor parties I have ever been to. My brother's was crazy and I don't remember much of it. Colin's was also insane and you never want to get into a drinking contest with a Scottish man; you *will* lose," he assured us. Thatch and I both chuckled. "Plus, I think I'm too old for that stuff anymore, anyway. I have a kid and another on the way and honestly I just want to be in bed before midnight most nights."

"Well, you might not get midnight tonight buddy," I clapped him on the shoulder. "We've got this place until two."

"That's okay. Stella's parents have Elsie tonight, so we can at least sleep in tomorrow."

"You still on the baby train?" I asked Thatch.

"Sort of. We're not exactly trying, but we're also not exactly preventing."

"Damn. Look at you guys all settled down. Maybe I need to, too."

Gabe and Thatch both shot me the same wide-eyed expression. "What?" asked Gabe. "You?"

"What? Is it really so hard to believe that I could settle down?"

"No. I guess not," added Thatch. "People change. Well, if you want the whole marriage and kids thing, I wholeheartedly support it. It's a pretty nice life."

"Yeah, kids are so weird though," added Gabe. "So be prepared for that. Owen already knows what it's like living with a baby and a toddler, but you'll be going in blind."

"Whoa, whoa. No one is having a baby right now—except you," I motioned to Gabe. "I'm just saying I'm starting to see something different for my future. I think I want the whole domestic life one day." They both drunkenly smiled at me.

"Okay, but for a whole, week Elsie wouldn't go to bed unless I gave her a marshmallow to hold. She didn't even want to eat it, just hold it to fall asleep. Then I'd take it away from her and save it for the next night. Next it was my stud finder," added Gabe.

"Oh yeah. I remember that," smiled Thatch.

Kids are weird. But I was also weird for suddenly thinking about Olivia being the mother of mine.

~ 13 ~

Olivia

"Okay, so nobody gives a shit about Owen and me getting married. We all just need the dirty details of you and Jake," began Greya when we were sitting in the steam room of the spa after our massages. "This is a safe space, I swear. None of this will get back to Owen. Everyone here is a vault. Right?" she glanced at her cousin Holly, who was just a couple of years younger than me.

"Yup," called Stella from her chair outside of the steam room door. "What is said in this steam room, stays in this steam room. None of this will get back to Gabe, I swear." Luckily, we were the only ones in there at the moment.

"There's not much to tell," I shrugged.

"Bullshit. We have all seen that man. There's stuff to tell," added Stella, pulling open the door slightly and calling in to us.

Greya just smiled at me as if to say, *she has a point.*

"Okay, maybe there's some stuff to tell. I called off our deal with helping me seeing as I quit my job. And…and I guess we're dating now."

Stella came into the steam room after that. "Okay, spill everything, but be quick. I can only be in here for about ten minutes," she added, patting her large baby belly.

"I mean, I think that's kind of it," I shrugged.

"How is he in bed?" asked Stella.

"Stella, you can't ask her that!" Greya interjected.

"Why not? We all want to know."

"Honestly, I wouldn't know. We've only been officially together for about a week. We haven't done anything yet."

Their mouths dropped. Even Holly, who really had no player in this game and was just along for the ride. She didn't even know the guy. "What?" I asked.

"I'm sorry. You expect us to believe that Jake Ellis has not slept with you yet?" said Stella.

"Well, it's true." I didn't exactly want to reveal the whole virgin thing to them.

"Okay," said Stella slightly leaning back on her hands and making her belly rounder. "Good for him, I guess. Maybe he's scared to sleep with you though, because of Owen."

"I don't think that's it," I replied. "He clearly made his choice to risk his friendship with Owen for me. I don't think that's why he's holding back. And we're not actually holding back, we just haven't gotten to that yet."

"Okay," Greya jumped in. "So, how is everything else though? What is Jake like as a boyfriend?"

"He's great, honestly."

"So when was the breaking point? When did you guys finally go from a fake relationship to more? It was the retreat, right?"

"Um, sort of. We did kiss at the retreat and got stuck sharing a bed—"

"Ha, classic," smiled Greya.

"But, then we got into a fight and it didn't start until I quit my job actually."

"Okay. But I'm guessing he's an amazing kisser," added Stella.

I instantly flushed, but I'm not sure anyone could tell because of the steam room. My automatic smile might have given it away though. "Uh, yeah, you could say that."

"Ugh, I miss the beginnings of a new relationship when every touch feels so igniting and you want each other all the time. Then before you know it, you're married and pregnant and find everything your husband does obnoxiously annoying and repulsive." We all stared at her. "Oh, no; I love Gabe, it's just the hormones. That man can really piss me off lately."

We all slightly laughed. "Well, it sounds like you guys really have something," said Greya. "I haven't known Jake for long, but I have never seen him like this before. Even when he was just fake dating you, he seemed more committed to you than I have ever seen him with any other girl. And it's not out of fear of what Owen might do. I can see the way he looks at you. I think you made an impression three years ago when you kissed him and he never got over it."

"Yeah, he kind of said that himself."

"Okay, I have to get out of here now," said Stella, heading for the door. "I think it's also getting to be time for our pedicures."

After our spa day, we all had dinner at this sushi place. It was Greya's favourite and we had booked a private room. The conversation about Jake and me had continued on into dinner, even with every attempt I made at trying to talk about someone else's love life. But Stella was kind of right. She and Greya were both essentially settled down and there was nothing new and exciting to talk about. No sparks flying, no sexual tension. Holly was single, so she couldn't come to my rescue either and drag the conversation in another direction. I finally did manage to get them talking about other things and Greya was soon showing me photos on her phone of the fancy resort she and Owen were planning on going to for their honeymoon. They were going to spend three weeks in Greece next summer when hockey season was done and the resort looked like a literal paradise on earth.

"I just wish Owen would let me book it in the next few months, but depending on if they make it to the playoffs or not, we might go at a different time. I get it. If they don't make it, we could go a lot sooner and miss the peak summer tourist season, but we could also just book it for when hockey season is for sure over," said Greya after popping a cucumber maki into her mouth.

"Well, it's not like it needs to be planned now. You have lots of time," I shrugged.

"Yeah, I guess. I just like things to be planned out and done. I don't really like leaving it up to the last minute."

"It won't be the last minute. You'll still have plenty of time to book the best honeymoon ever."

"I know. I just really want it to be special…"

I could get the sense that there was something more there than what she was saying. "Hey," began Stella. "It will be the best honeymoon you've ever been on, because it'll be with Owen and you love him."

"I know," she smiled at her. I had known about the fact that Greya's first husband died only a couple of months after they got married, so I'm guessing that she maybe never got to go on a honeymoon with him.

"I've always wanted to go to Greece," chimed in Holly. "You're going to have so much fun. Can you take me instead?" she joked.

"Sure. Then we can go during hockey season," she bantered back.

When I got home from my day with the girls, I collapsed onto my couch. It wasn't late, seeing as our dinner was more lupper, but I was somehow still exhausted and glad to be home. I knew the guys were still out partying and probably just getting to their dinner, but I checked my phone anyway for any sign that Jake was thinking of me too. As if he was summoned, when I picked up my phone a message from him came in.

Jake: *Having fun?*

Me: *Yeah, just got home. You?*

Jake: *Oh yeah. We're just headed to the steakhouse for dinner now.*

Me: *Sounds yummy. Have a good time. Maybe I'll talk to you later if you're not too inebriated to function.*

Jake: *Why GT, I would never get so drunk to the point of not being able to hold a coherent conversation with you.*

Me: *Sure *eye roll emoji*. But it is my brother's bachelor party, so you should go as wild as you want to.*

Jake: *See this is why I like you. You don't try to turn me into someone I'm not.*

Me: *That's what you think. If I do it properly, you'll never know it happened in the first place *winky face emoji**

Jake: *Is that a promise?*

Me: *You'll have to wait and see, but text me when you're done living it up and maybe I'll let you come over if you're not ready to end the night.*

Jake: *I will definitely be texting you.*

I must have fallen asleep on my couch while watching TV. I was in a blissful sushi/spa coma and I didn't want to be roused from it. My phone seemed to have other plans though, and I finally dragged myself to sitting and pulled my phone from the coffee table. It was twelve-forty a.m.

Jake: *Hey, you're probably asleep, but I'm heading home and I figured I'd see if you happened to be up.*

Me: *Lucky for you, I actually am. I took a nap, so I'm all rested. Aren't you exhausted though?*

Jake: *Me? Never.*

Me: *Well, I guess come on over if you want to then.*

Jake: *Be there in fifteen.*

Then my stomach growled. I guess the sushi wasn't there anymore.

Me: *Weird request, but can you bring me a burger? And onion rings?*

Jake: *Sure.*

Jake was at my door half an hour later with burger in hand. I think I was falling in love with that man. The quickest way to a woman's heart is to bring her food in the middle of the night.

"How was the bachelor party?" I asked after my first bite of burger. Jake was sitting across from me, snacking on one of my onion rings.

"It was great. Your brother is completely hammered and I don't think Benny liked me that much when I dropped him off at their place."

I smiled. "She'll forgive you. You're annoyingly loveable."

"Yeah, is that what you think of me?"

"Maybe. You definitely managed to sway my opinion away from utter loathing to pleasantly liking," I gave him a wry smile through my last mouthful of burger.

"Utter loathing, huh?" He leaned back in his chair, "Well, I guess you know what they say. Lust and hate have a very thin line between them. But," he leaned forward, "we're going to have to work on this only 'pleasantly liking' bit."

I swallowed and my heart rate quickened. Okay, I definitely more than pleasantly liked that man, but he was also really fun to tease. He stood from his chair and walked over to me, bracing a hand on the table in front of me and leaning into my space. He pushed my empty plate out of the way and crouched down to my level, then with one quick movement—and a body-melting devilish smirk—he pulled me from my seat and sat me on the table in front of him, wedging his large hips between my parted knees. His lips were soon on mine and I was breathing him in; his warm mouth, with a subtle hint of alcohol, but not too much seeing as he did just drive. He grabbed either side of my hips and dragged them closer to the edge of the table and started to lay me back on it. He was on top of me and I wanted so much more of him. I was clawing at his shirt and his hair, anything I could find to try to bring him that much closer to me. He finally pulled me back up and lifted me off the table, carrying me over to the bedroom and sitting me on the edge of my bed. Then he just looked at me.

"Why did you stop?" I asked him.

"Because it's one-thirty in the morning and we should both probably get some rest."

"I don't want you to stop," I pleaded with him, the ache in me still craving his touch.

"Believe me GT, I definitely don't *want* to stop. But that doesn't mean we shouldn't."

"Well, you can still sit next to me," I said, motioning to the spot on the bed beside me. "We can still just lay here for a bit."

"If I get into that bed with you, I have no idea where it'll go."

"Well, you managed to keep your hands off of me during the retreat and we shared a bed."

"Yeah, not very well," he pointed out.

I stood on the bed and placed my feet right on the edge of it, reaching out for him and pulling him closer to me. We were now the same height. I wrapped my arms around his neck and pressed my body to his. "I think you can lie here next to me for a minute without it leading to anything."

He let out a sigh and lifted my legs around his waist, then fell to the bed with me underneath him. I let out a small laugh as he kissed my neck. Then he rolled me on top of him and pulled my lips to his with a fistful of my hair. We stayed that way for a while, switching who was on top until we finally did stop and just laid next to one another.

When the sun crested over the horizon, I was briefly awoken and glanced over at Jake, sound asleep laying on his stomach, still in his clothes from the night before, clutching my pillow with both arms. I nudged closer to him and he stirred slightly, just enough to move from his stomach to his side and pull me into him.

A few hours later, we were waking together once again. I looked at my phone and it was almost noon.

"Wow, we really slept in," I yawned.

"Yeah. I don't think I've slept this late in a long time," he replied. "I do have to get going though," he said, placing a small kiss on my forehead. "I wish we could do breakfast or something, but I actually have to pick up my suit for the wedding in half an hour."

"Oh, no problem," I smiled. "I guess I will see you there then."

"Yeah." He paused a moment and looked at me, a devious grin coming onto his face. "Now, how far do you think we can take it without your brother freaking out? A drink? A dance maybe?"

"Probably not even that."

"Well, there goes making-out in the bathroom then," he shrugged. "I guess I'll have to settle for just being able to look at you any chance I get."

~ 14 ~

Jake

There I was, back in Aspen at Thatch's place. They were having a small wedding in the backyard of his cabin and the whole event went off without a hitch. Benny must have worn him down because I did end up walking down the aisle with Olivia, but not before I got a stern warning from him about touching his sister—oops.

The ceremony was beautiful though, and it honestly made me think that maybe one day I wanted that too. Marriage was never something on my mind until I knew how it felt to be with someone who made you as happy as Olivia made me.

"The Best" by Tina Turner played the moment Benny and Thatch locked lips for their first kiss, and I took the opportunity to glance over at Olivia. I figured he was pretty distracted and wouldn't notice me eye-fucking his sister.

We kept our distance at the reception, but the way she looked in her bridesmaid dress only made me want to sneak her away somewhere private so I could rip her out of it. I was being patient and waiting, though. I was going to do things right with her.

I managed to find her at the bar—it seemed like an innocent place to run into her that no one would suspect any foul play from.

"Hey," I smiled when I stood beside her.

"Hi," she turned and smiled at me.

"I think everything's going really well," I added after ordering a drink.

"Yeah, it is. The ceremony was beautiful and I think my brother may have lightened up a bit."

My nose crinkled and my lips pursed, "Uh, I wouldn't say that. The talking-to he gave me before the ceremony about keeping my hands off you would suggest otherwise."

"Oh, sorry."

I shrugged. "It's fine. I can just put them on you later when we're alone."

"Shhh," she whispered.

"Hey guys," Benny interrupted us.

"Oh, hey," smiled Olivia.

"So, what are *you* two talking about over here?"

"Oh nothing. Just debating on whether my brother is going to go for the face or the gut when he punches Jake."

She chuckled, "Yeah, well, you're lucky he's decently drunk and distracted right now," Benny added.

"Benny, it was a beautiful ceremony, and you look gorgeous as always," I chimed in. "Oh, wait. Am I going to have to stop calling you that now? Is it Thatch now too? Damn, there's too many of you," I glanced at Olivia. "Mrs. Thatch, maybe?" I joked.

"I don't entirely hate the sound of that," she joked back, "but I'm not sure I'm even changing my last name yet, so the nickname can stay for now."

"Well if you do…" I leaned into Olivia and whispered in her ear, "Or, I'll just have to come up with some other nickname for you. Something that suits you better—" Benny cleared her throat. "Well, I'm going to go then," I said, taking my drink. "Got to keep my distance."

I headed for my table, leaving the girls to chat. I knew they were almost certainly talking about me.

"Hey, man," greeted Gabe sitting next to me. He had his daughter with him. She looked pretty cute as their flower girl.

"Hey," I answered, taking a sip of my drink.

"Having a good time?"

"Yeah. You?"

"Oh, yeah. I mean it could be more fun if I didn't have this one with me, but Stella's parents will take her back to the hotel soon. Then we can party," he added.

"Hey!" interrupted his daughter.

"Honey, I love you, but sometimes grown-ups want to have fun without kids around. You get to hang out with your grandparents and you're going to have way more fun."

"Yes!" said Elsie with a little fist pump.

I just smiled and took another sip of my drink.

"So, still seeing whatever girl has been occupying all of your time?" asked Gabe.

"Hmm? Oh yeah. Uh, yeah, it's going well."

"Uh-huh," smiled Gabe.

"What?"

"Nothing. Just never seen you so preoccupied by a girl before. The same girl, actually. I should clarify."

I shot him a glare, "Yeah, well, things change."

"Yeah, they do."

"So when do we all get to meet her?"

"One day. Now's not the right time."

"Why? You still unsure?"

"Nope. Actually I've never been more sure of anything in my life. It's just a bit complicated. Don't worry, though, you'll all get to find out who the mystery girl is eventually."

"What mystery girl?" interjected Stella.

"Oh, Ellis has some girl he's been hiding from everyone."

"Nice," smiled Stella. Then she turned to her daughter. "Okay, Grandma's here. Time to go."

"Yay!" Elsie bounced off her dad's lap and headed out.

"Well, it sounds like this girl is something, if she got you to settle down," continued Gabe.

"Hey, I'm not settled down—yet."

"Uh-huh," he smirked.

We were suddenly interrupted by Benny getting everyone's attention, as she and Thatch stood on the dance floor. "Hello, everyone," she began. "We just wanted to thank you all for being here tonight to celebrate with us. As many of you may know, Owen and I didn't exactly start off on the right foot, but eventually I forgave him for being a hockey player,"—the crowd laughed—"and our friendship grew into something more, and now I'm lucky enough to get to call him not only my friend but my husband."

Thatch took the mic from her after giving her a quick kiss on the cheek. "Yes, thank you all for being here. I consider myself the luckiest man on earth to get to call this woman my wife and not to put a damper on this celebration, but we wouldn't be standing here today if it weren't for some tragic circumstances, so we wanted to take a moment to remember the reason why I got the privilege of falling in love with this woman, and make a to toast to Colin. I didn't know you, but I promise I'm taking good care of her for you."

Fuck. Why is it that those two can always make me almost want to cry?

Everyone raised their glasses and drank. Then Thatch continued, "But now, on a happier note, let's get this party started!" He pulled Benny into a kiss and music started playing as he led her around the dance floor. I wished I could pull Olivia onto it also, but that was definitely risky. I would have to settle for stealing small glances throughout the night and hopefully getting to see her later.

***

I was back in my hotel room after the wedding. I had got there maybe ten minutes before there was a knock on my door.

"Hey," I smiled when I saw Olivia on the other side of it.

"Hi," she smiled, then let herself in. "You look super sexy right now," she drawled, moving closer to me and pulling me to her from the lapels of my suit jacket. We locked lips for a moment.

"Yeah? You look pretty sexy too," I placed my hands on her hips. "You have no idea how many times I imagined sneaking you away tonight."

"Well, I'm here now. What do you want to do to me?"

Everything. So much. "Nah, you're far too drunk for that," I smiled.

"I am not."

"Yes, you are. But, I will still make-out with you on the bed for a bit."

She smirked and then slowly backed herself over to the bed, not breaking her eye contact with me the entire time. I took off my jacket and tossed it on the chair, then strode over to the bed to meet her, rolling my sleeves up on my forearms. She sat on it and I nudged her legs apart with my knee, then lowered myself over her and met her lips with mine. God, those lips. I could kiss them all day every day. We moved back onto the bed more until we were lying down and our bodies hugged each other as I kissed every exposed inch of her. I wanted to rip off that dress so badly and have my way with her, but she was drunk and I was not going to let her first time be this way. So I controlled myself—and her. She was incredibly handsy and it took all my willpower to pull her hands away from my pants.

"We should slow down," I breathed when I managed to pry my lips from hers for a moment.

"I don't want to."

"Olivia, you don't want it to be this way. Believe me. We can wait."

"Fine," she sighed. "Can I stay here tonight though? I promise I'll keep my hands off you," she giggled. "Imagine *me* having to keep my hands off of *you*," she giggled again.

Fuck she was sexy.

"Alright. You want to go change and then come back?"

"No." She got off the bed and stood in front of me. Then reached for the zipper on her dress and unzipped it, letting her dress fall to the floor.

Ah, fuck. She was standing there in a strapless bra and these little sexy booty shorts. "I'll get you a t-shirt," I said, getting off the bed too.

"What? As if you haven't been wanting to see this?"

"Yeah, but not tonight."

"Yes, and I agreed to that, so turn around," she teased, taking the shirt from me.

"No," I crossed my arms against my chest.

"Fine," she smirked with a devilish gleam in her eyes. Then she reached behind her and undid her bra.

Fuuucck!

She put my shirt on right after that, but it was too late. I saw them and all I wanted to do was know what they felt like in my hands. I closed the gap between us and lifted her up and back onto the bed. As I moved over her, my hand brushed up her hip, over her belly and up her shirt. My lips followed, trailing kisses all up her.

"Mmmm," she moaned.

Fuck. I was being such a goddamn gentleman.

~ 15 ~

Olivia

Jake's arms held me tight through the night and I awoke the next morning completely safe and content in them. My head was on his chest and his fingers were tangled in my hair, gently playing with it as he drifted in and out of sleep.

"Good morning," I smiled when I managed to pull myself off him and turn slightly to meet his lips with mine.

"Good morning," he smiled back. "How is it possible you look even sexier first thing in the morning? No makeup and messy hair."

I propped myself up on my elbows and kissed his chest. "Hey, thanks for not letting me do anything stupid last night," I said. He raised a brow at me. "Not that sex with you would be stupid. It'd be great, I'm sure, but—"

"I know what you meant, GT. Don't worry. And it would be fucking mind-blowing, just to let you know. Best you've ever had."

"You know I have nothing to compare it to," I mocked.

"Yeah, so it'll be the best. I'm just going to tell you right now, it doesn't get better than me."

"Uh-huh. Anyway, thanks again," I kissed him. "But, I am very sober now…" I added, dragging my fingertips closer to the waistline of his pants.

"I don't think so. It's not the right time."

"Really?" I questioned with a raised brow.

"I didn't bring any protection."

"I find it hard to believe that you don't just always have some in your suitcase."

"Well, I don't."

"Uh-huh, sure. Well, I'm on birth control."

He let out a heavy sigh, "Ugh, you have no idea how hard it is for me to be saying no to you right now."

"Oh, I can see how hard it is…and it's not like I've never done *anything* before…"

He reacted instantly and I looked up at him. He reached down and took my hand away from his pants and then flipped us so he was on top of me. He gently placed kisses from my hips all the way up, removing my shirt as he went. He tossed it to the floor and pinned my hands above my head and devoured me with his lips on mine. The passion exuding from him was unmatched as he drove his hips into me so I could feel just how into my proposition he was. When he finally released my hands and moved his to my hair, I moved mine to his pants and slowly found my way inside. He let out a primal groan as I moved over him.

Jake pulled me into a steamy shower after and gave me a taste of what being with him would be like. When we were done, I headed back to my room to change and then we decided to meet for breakfast. There was a very slim chance we would run into anyone. Greya and Owen were at their cabin and we didn't really need to hide from anyone else—except maybe my parents.

"Shit!" I called out when we were walking down the street.

"What?" asked Jake.

"My parents are coming this way." I grabbed his hand and pulled him into the shop next to us. We watched as they walked by and then headed out of the shop and walked in the opposite direction. "That was close," I said.

After breakfast, we said our goodbyes and each headed back to the city. Pre-season was starting soon, so Jake was going to be busier for the next few weeks, but we still made plans to see each other as much as we could. I suppose that was one plus of being unemployed; I could see my boyfriend as much as I wanted.

***

"Hey, you're coming to the game tomorrow, right?" asked Owen when I was at his place a few weeks later.

"Yeah, I'll be there," I smiled.

"Good, I need some company," added Greya. "Stella's busy with a newborn, so it would just be me and while I *love* watching you play," she teased my brother, "I do like having someone to talk to." She moved closer to me and whispered, "I hate hockey wives, so I don't sit with them."

"Thanks, babe. I feel so loved," Owen grinned.

"Hey, you knew this about me when you married me," added Greya.

"Yeah, but I figured after three years together, I would have finally won you over on hockey players," he added, heading off to the kitchen. A moment later he called out to us, "Hey, Liv, Jake is texting you." Shit! I left my phone on their counter. Greya and I froze. "Wow, a lot. Who's Jake?"

Oh my God. He actually wasn't cluing in. Thank God hockey players basically forget people even have first names.

"Oh, um, just someone I went to school with," I casually said as I headed for the kitchen and took my phone from the counter. "He might have a job opportunity for me, so it's probably about that."

"Oh, sweet. Well, hopefully it all works out."

"Yeah, I hope so. I've been pretty bored not working."

"And you're still fine money wise?" he asked.

"Yes, Owen, I have savings and I'm fine."

"Okay, okay," he put his hands up in surrender. "Cause you just bought that new car, so if you need help with payments or anything. I'm just making sure my baby sister isn't going to be forced to live on the street."

I rolled my eyes. "That wouldn't happen. I'd just move in with you guys," I shot a smile back at Greya. "Well," I sighed, "I should go. I'll see you tomorrow. Kick ass on the ice or whatever," I added to Owen.

The next night I was at the arena with Greya watching the players warm up on the ice and seeing Jake do his stretches before the game was causing some problems for me. I was trying really hard not to imagine his hips doing that to me rather than the ice.

"You okay over there?" interrupted Greya as she snapped me out of it.

"What? Yeah, I'm fine. Totally fine."

"The appeal wears off, you'll get used to it," she assured me. "I basically never even look at Owen warming up anymore. I do, however, watch all of the other women here watching him. It feels really good knowing you have what they want," she lifted her brows at me.

Colorado was winning, but honestly, we weren't really watching.

"So, how *are* things with Jake?" she asked me.

"Good. Really good actually."

"That's great. See, I told you to go for it."

"That's not really what happened," I replied.

"I mean, it's basically what happened."

"If it weren't for my boss being his biggest fan, none of this would have happened."

"I suppose. But you never know, it might have. And for all of your boss's downfalls, I guess you can at least thank him for this," she joked.

"Yeah, I guess."

Then the crowd around us seemly did a collective, "Awww," and I looked up to see the clip of Greya and Owen on the big screen.

"Damn, I need to steal that tape," groaned Greya.

I just chuckled. "Ah, come on. It's cute."

"Well, hey, maybe you two could do that and then it won't be me up there anymore."

"I don't think so. I'm sure people would brush past the kiss and only remember my brother beating him into the ice."

"Maybe. But, look. He really only wants what's best for you, and if that's Jake, then he'll come around. Whenever you guys are ready to tell him, I will be in your corner. Just let me know ahead of time. I'll put him in a really good mood first," she winked.

"Gross," I scrunched my face. "But thanks. You're the best sister-in-law I could ask for."

After the game, I headed home. I didn't feel like sticking around with Greya to meet Owen and I knew that seeing Jake after would result in me wanting to meet him at his place and I had to get a good night's sleep. Even though we weren't having sex, he still managed to keep me awake far later than I should be most nights.

Me: *Hey, good game.*

Jake: *Thanks. Maybe one day you'll actually get to be wearing my number.*

Me: *Hopefully. Greya is fully on board with reigning in Owen when we decide to break the news.*

Jake: *You want to come over tonight? But you better not still be wearing your brother's jersey when you do. That will be weird.*

Me: *Tempting, but I'm pretty tired. I think I just want to head home. I have an interview tomorrow I want to prep for.*

Jake: *Well, good luck. They'd be stupid not to hire you.*

Me: *Thanks.*

***

The interview did not go well. They asked way too many questions about why I quit my last job. It was completely unfathomable to them that I would give up the opportunity to be working with Carter Callaghan. Now I was still unemployed and I only had so many savings until I would be forced to move, or just get whatever job I could to pay the bills.

Jake was putting forkfuls of food into his mouth as I sat across from him at his place for dinner. I had barely touched my meal because my mind kept wandering. Things were going great with him, but I was starting to wonder why he was holding back when it came to sex. It had been weeks now since Owen and Greya's wedding and since then, we had definitely gotten a lot more familiar with each other, but he still wasn't taking my v-card. I was starting to wonder if there was something wrong with me.

~ 16 ~

Jake

"Dude, what's with you lately?" asked Thatch in the locker room after the game. We were about to head out, and I knew that Greya was waiting for him.

"What?" I asked, pulling my shirt over my head.

"You're different. And I think it has something to do with whatever girl has been taking up all of your time."

"It's nothing, really," I tried to brush him off.

"Really? Nothing? Come on, man. It's me. Do you have a girlfriend? Is it that same girl you mentioned at my bachelor party?"

I shot my head back. "Me? No."

"Yes you do. You totally have a girlfriend."

I sighed, "Fine. I might be seeing someone."

"Who is she? When do we get to meet her?"

"You don't get to know anything about her. Not yet, anyway."

"Okay, fine. Well, it's really nice to see you like this."

"Like what?"

"All happy and shit. And a girl is making you this way. You're like a lovesick puppy."

"I. Am. Not." I was though. But I had to keep the ruse up. Olivia was definitely making me feel all the puppy love crap and I didn't hate it. I had no idea this was what I was missing out on all this time.

"Yes you are, and it's nice to see you this way." He threw his bag over his shoulder. "Well, whoever she is, she's lucky. You're one of the best guys I know even if you don't show it a lot of the time. When we finally do get to meet her, I'm sure we'll all love her if you do."

The season had started. I was on the ice basically every day and Olivia had pretty much moved in with me by the amount she was at my place, but I didn't mind. It meant that I could still see her as much as I wanted. She was staying over almost every night, but she was also busy with job hunting.

"You know," she said one night when she was straddling my lap on my couch. "I think we should do it. It's been long enough and I am very ready."

"Uh-uh," I shook my head.

"What? Okay, seriously, Jake? I'm starting to think that it's me. Are you changing your mind or something?"

"No. God no. It's just…"

"What? What is it?" She was getting annoyed and for good reason. "I find it really hard to believe that you, the guy who basically has a different girl every week is not in the mood to go upstairs and—"

"Okay, why does everyone keep thinking that about me?" I cut her off.

"What? Because that's who you are. I don't care if that's what you're worried about. Obviously I don't because I'm with you, but…"

"Look, Liv, I'm going to level with you. I'm not this sex crazed player that everyone thinks I am. There used to

193

be maybe a new girl every month, but I really didn't get around as much as everyone thinks."

"Then why do you let everyone think you do?"

"I don't know. There was this one time where I dated a few girls back to back and since then everyone just thinks that's my normal. Trying to say it's not has never gotten me anywhere so I just let them believe it now. It doesn't harm me," I shrugged. "But look, the truth is that I was nineteen when I lost my virginity, which apparently is kinda old for a guy, and I did just do it to get it over with and I don't want that for you. I want to be able to…"

"Be able to what?" She looked me in the eye, with her intense blue irises.

I took a breath. "I want to be able to tell you that I love you before, during, and after. Because that's what you deserve." Damn. I was used to spewing some BS, I love you crap to get a girl into bed, not keep one out of it. I was just hoping she didn't think that was just some line. Because there was no way I would risk the wrath of Owen Thatcher if I wasn't one-hundred percent certain about her. This wasn't just some game to me; this was end game for me. And I knew she felt it too. We both knew it the moment I said 'fuck it' in that shower and kissed her stupid, but that other stuff, it just didn't quite feel like the right move for us yet. But that next fuck it moment was going to be legendary.

That moment when I take her every which way I want because she's wholly mine and we both know it.

She didn't say anything for a moment, then quietly, "Okay then. We can wait." She kissed me softly and I pulled her into me. We stayed that way for a moment. "Hey!" she suddenly called out. "Wait… How did you do that? I didn't even feel it," she felt under her shirt.

I just smirked. She then took the straps of her bra off and pulled the whole thing off under her t-shirt. "You may as well just take the whole thing off," I teased.

"No, I don't know," she teased back, getting off my lap and backing up. "I think you're going to have to work for it."

"Is that so?" I asked, getting to my feet and making my way slowly over to her. She backed up slightly, then bolted for the stairs. I caught her and threw her over my shoulder and carried her up to my bedroom, where that shirt was definitely coming off.

***

Olivia was at my place applying for jobs on her laptop while I was in the kitchen making dinner. Yes, I can cook, I just don't like to. I liked cooking for her, though.

"Hey," I called out. "Why don't you come to Vegas this weekend? You can watch the game and then be waiting for me in my hotel room."

"Really?" her head turned to me.

"Yeah, you're unemployed now. What else do you have to do?"

"I don't know. Look for a job."

"I'm rich; you don't need one. Anyway, it'll be fun and it's not like you'll be going to interviews or anything on the weekend."

"And how do you suppose you're going to hide me from Owen?" She was heading to the kitchen at that point.

"Don't worry about it," I grinned.

"I don't know. It does sound fun, but it also sounds very risky."

"Come on. Take the risk, it'll be worth it," I flashed her a sexy grin that I knew made her melt.

She bit her lower lip and then thought for a moment. "Okay," she smiled.

***

Me: *Okay, the front desk has your name. Just give them your ID when you get there and they'll give you a key to my room.*

GT: *Okay. Good luck tonight *kissy face emoji**

Me: *Thanks, baby doll. But you know I don't need luck *winky face emoji**

GT: **Eye roll emoji**

Our game went very well. Maybe Olivia was my good luck charm. We beat them five to one and I was still riding that high when I unlocked my hotel room door to find Olivia there waiting for me. I walked into the room and she ran up to me, jumping into my arms, wrapping her legs around my waist and kissing me.

"That was insane!" she said. "Probably one of the best games I've been to in a while."

"Thanks. It was all for you, babe."

"Yeah, you were showing off for me?"

"Maybe just a little," I grinned while walking us over to the bed and throwing her down onto it. I then climbed onto it beside her and pulled her to me. "So, what do you feel like doing? Want to go out?"

"Oh...I kind of figured we'd have to stay in the room all night. You don't want to risk anyone seeing us."

"Well, the *'anyone'* in particular that you are talking about is pretty preoccupied right now. Believe me. Benny called when he was getting out of the elevator, so he'll be busy for a while. They're probably having phone sex or something."

"Eww, that's my brother!"

"Sorry. I meant he's all boring and committed now, so he'll probably be in all night. He doesn't party anymore."

"Uh-huh," she sighed. "Well, I am pretty hungry, so I guess if you're sure no one will see us..."

~ 17 ~

Olivia

We burst through Jake's hotel room door hours later, a little buzzed, a little happy, and a little, oh yeah...

Married.

Yeah. We got married.

Jake carried me over to the bed like his bride and laid me down on it. It didn't take him long to be on top of me, claiming my lips with his. His kisses were hot and desperate and I knew that he wasn't going to hold back this time. Every kiss from him was sending tingles through my body as he ripped every piece of clothing from me. I did the same to him until we were naked under the covers and our bodies were melting into one another. I had been waiting for this moment for a long time. When he finally broke down his walls and let me in fully—or rather, him in, I guess.

"See," he said, breaking our kiss for a moment, "look at you waiting for marriage and all. You are a good girl," he teased.

"You know. I think you're actually the one that made me wait. I was ready to do this last week. Was this your plan all along? So you'd be able to rub my good girl reputation in my face?"

"No," he smiled back. "Last week I was only ninety-nine percent sure I loved you. Now I'm one thousand percent sure," he said, capturing my lips with his again.

"Wow, you go from ninety-nine to one thousand pretty quickly"

"Yeah I do," he wiggled his brows suggestively. "So, Mrs. Ellis…" He paused, a slow smile growing on his lips. "Hmm…Olivia Ellis. Now that name I like the sound of."

"It does have a nice ring to it."

He pulled me on top of him and grabbed a fistful of my hair, bringing my lips back to his. We stayed that way for a moment, just moving with one another. "Fuck, I love you," he groaned as my hips rocked over him. "Are you ready for more, though?" he asked, flipping me over and positioning himself on top of me. I nodded. Staring into his grey, ocean blue eyes, I wanted nothing more than to feel all of him. I was so ready for him. He went slowly and made sure that everything he was doing was comfortable for me, but I was surprised at how badly I wanted more of him. Eventually we found our rhythm and he was thrusting his hips against me harder and harder and making sounds that only spurred my desire for him. I had never felt anything like it and I knew that I was going to be addicted to that feeling for life; the feeling of Jake Ellis between my legs and of being his wife.

"Holy fuck!" he breathed out when we were laying in bed together after. "That was probably the best sex I've ever had."

"You're just saying that."

"Nope, I'm serious." He leaned down and kissed me. "You're amazing and I will never get sick of that." I giggled. He then reached for his phone on the nightstand.

"What are you doing?" I asked.

"Just changing your name in my phone." I looked at his phone screen and saw 'Wifey' with a little heart emoji next to it.

"Aww, who would have taken you as the type to have that in your phone."

"I know, right? I guess I just hadn't met the right girl yet. Well, actually I did meet her before, but it was complicated so I had to let the idea of her go. I guess you're a good substitute."

"Mmhmm," I mumbled, snuggling into him even more and laying my head on his chest.

He dragged his fingers through my hair, "You good? Sore at all?"

"Nope, I'm great," I smiled.

"Good. You should probably go pee though," he added.

I giggled again, "Thanks. You know I may have never done that before, but I'm not completely uneducated. I do know that at least," I said, getting up from the bed.

"Hey, just making sure my wife doesn't get a UTI."

"Well, thank you," I said kissing him again and giving him a little hip wiggle as I walked over to the bathroom.

When I headed back into the bedroom, seeing Jake in bed waiting for me and everything that had happened, kind of all hit me at once and the panic started to set in.

I married my brother's best friend and he doesn't even know about it.

"What's wrong?" asked Jake when he saw me. "Shit, what happened?"

"Nothing," I said going over to him and climbing into the bed then wiping away a few tears that managed to break through the surface.

"Shit. My mom always used to tell me to 'ruin her lipstick, not her mascara' and I've always tried pretty hard to live my life that way, but now you're crying…"

"I'm not really crying. I'm fine. And it has nothing to do with you. Well, not really. It just all hit me all of a sudden that we're married and we're going to have to tell people eventually and…"

"Hey," he pulled me close to him. "We've got this, and these are bridges to cross when the time is right. It will all work out, you know it will. And we have each other to get through it."

"Thanks. I know." I stayed there in his arms for a moment, embracing the feeling of his strong grasp around me. "Your mom seems really great that she used to give you that advice about girls. I can't wait to meet her one day. My mom used to tell me to, 'be the girl he practiced for, not the one he practiced on'. I guess maybe that played into the whole virgin thing. Who knows?"

"Your mom is pretty cool, and she already loves me," he teased. "But yeah, my mom's a great mom. She got pregnant when she was sixteen and we were on our own for a long time. She finished high school and then nursing school all with a little kid and the hospital where she worked was where she met my step-dad. He's a cardiothoracic surgeon."

"Wow."

"Yeah. If the hockey thing didn't work out, I was headed for med-school too."

"What? Really?" I sat up and looked at him.

He nodded, "Uh-huh."

"So that's where the whole shower burn thing came from?"

"No, that's just basic first-aid. Everyone should know that."

"Alright, well, I can't wait to meet your family when the time comes. Maybe we can use them as a trial run for when we tell my brother."

"Sure, sounds good."

***

I moved in with Jake later that week. I was unpacking some more boxes while Jake was at practice when I decided it was time that I probably let someone in on what had happened. She was the only person who was going to be in our corner when it came time to tell my brother.

Me: *Okay, I might have done something impulsive.*

Greya: *What? Does this have to do with a certain hockey player?*

Me: *Maybe.*

Greya: *Spill, girl.*

Me: *Okay, so I met Jake in Vegas last weekend and...*

Greya: *And what? I think I know where this is going but you have to say it.*

Me: *We got married.*

She called me.

"WHAT?" she practically yelled into the phone when I answered.

"Yeah."

"Okay, how did that happen? I am also deleting all these messages so Owen doesn't see them."

"Thanks. Um, well, he invited me to Vegas for his game and then we went out after it and…got married. I don't really know what else to say."

"Was this a drunken thing that you guys now regret, or was this an intentional thing and you're living happily ever after?"

"The second one."

"Yes! See, I called it."

"Yeah…" I hoped she could hear the eye roll in my voice. "Anyway, we're probably going to have to tell Owen that we're together now. We're still not sure when the best time will be, but I'll let you know when we're ready."

"Okay, but I wouldn't wait too long now. He's going to be more pissed the longer you keep this from him."

"Do you think in any way, us being married will make him less angry? Like, we're not just fooling around. We do love each other and we're it for each other."

"Maybe. But he's probably going to think you're both being stupid because how can you know a few months into dating that they're the one?"

"You can though. I didn't believe it until I lived it."

"Hey, I get it, but I don't think there's anything you can do to soften the blow. I would just say do it sooner rather than later, but you probably also want to enjoy the honeymoon phase until it all comes crashing down on you."

"Yeah. Maybe they'll win the Cup this year and we can tell him after that. He'll be in a super good mood."

"I don't think you can wait that long," she pointed out.

"Probably not."

"Okay, well, I have to go, but holy shit! Congratulations!"

"Thanks."

~ 18 ~

Jake

Fuck, I loved married life. Well, sort of. I walked into my closet and it had been taken over by all of Olivia's things—mostly her shoes. That girl had a lot of heels. I didn't hate it; she was unbelievably sexy in them, but I was starting to think that we would need a bigger closet.

"How many shoes do you have? They're taking up half my closet."

She just flattened her lips and glared at me over her shoulder. "It's not that many. Relax. Plus, I need to look good for my brand new job."

Henry, her old co-worker, had called her earlier in the week and officially offered her a job with the new company he was starting. I was over-the-moon happy for her and it was so nice to see her excited about her job again. It wasn't going to start for a while though, and Henry still had a lot of things to work out, but the job was there for her when he was ready.

"Yeah, I guess I just have to get used to all of your things in my space now. I'm also working on getting used to your hair being everywhere. Seriously. What's with that?"

"Hey, you're the one that said mermaid length is the sexiest length. If you want it like this, you have to deal with the shedding. Also, it isn't even mermaid length. It barely covers my boobs, so just imagine how much more annoying it could be."

"All I heard was boobs."

She smiled back at me and rolled her eyes. "And you're the one whose hair is everywhere. When it's short and it sheds, it just falls on the floor. At least mine gets stuck in the rest and I just brush it out. You don't hear me complaining about having to deal with your messes, because I love you."

"Okay, fine." I watched her organizing the closet for another moment. "Hey, I want to show you something," I finally said.

"Huh? Okay."

"Come here," I motioned for her and she walked over to my outstretched hand and took it. I led her out of the closet and over to the bed where my laptop was. "Pick one," I pointed. She glanced at the screen to find a ring website up.

"What's this?" she asked, as if she didn't already know.

"You need a ring. I promised you I'd get you one and I want it to be something you love, so help me pick one."

She turned back to face me and smiled. "Okay." She took the computer and kneeled on the bed, moving to the headboard and sitting against it. Then she motioned for me to sit next to her. I did, and we sat together looking through the options. "None of these have prices," she pointed out.

"That's because it doesn't matter," I stated the obvious.

"I feel weird not knowing how much they are. What if I accidentally pick a million dollar ring?"

"Then you get a million dollar ring. But trust me, these won't even come close. I know you're not the type that needs a giant rock that everyone will stare at. Just like your car, I'm holding back, so it suits you."

She leaned over and kissed me. "Okay then." She kept scrolling through ring after ring and they were all starting to look the same to me. She finally did pick one and we even found one for me, too. I'm not going to lie; this was the first purchase I have ever made that gave me weird stomach flutters. I was excited to have something around my finger—and hers—that told the world we had chosen our person and we were together forever.

I closed my laptop and put it on the nightstand, "Well, now that that's done…" I moved closer to her and pulled her on top of me.

"I'm still trying to unpack."

"You can take a break."

She shook her head and crossed her arms. "I want to get it all done first and then I can relax. You already made me take a break for ring shopping."

"Fine," I sighed and playfully pushed her off me. "You can go finish unpacking. What do you want for dinner?"

"Whatever is fine."

"Okay."

***

That game was brutal. We won in the end but the other guys definitely made us work for it. I was sitting on the bench in the locker room when Thatch sat next to me. I knew Olivia was at the game with Benny, and all I wanted was to be able to go out there and grab her and kiss her like I knew Thatch was going to do with his wife. One day— hopefully. If I'm not dead.

I headed out after him and, just like I predicted, he scooped up his wife and spun her around, kissing her. Olivia was standing off to the side. I was surprised to actually see her there. She usually didn't stick around after the games. Maybe because she knows it drives me crazy seeing her in her brother's jersey and I can't wait until the day she can wear my last name with pride and show the world she chose me. I'm starting to come to terms with it, though; my last name is all over everything else she has now.

"Good game," Olivia smiled at her brother, but I knew she was mostly talking to me.

"Yeah, thanks." Thatch seemed to be less aware lately when his sister and I were in the same vicinity as one another and he seemed to just brush it off now, so hopefully we were making progress and when he finds out that I'm actually his brother-in-law, he'll be less up for assaulting me.

"Alright, I'm heading home," I said, clapping Thatch on the shoulder.

"Yes, I should go home too," smiled Olivia and only Benny gave us a look of suggesting if we were really going to risk walking out together.

"We'll walk with you guys," said Thatch as he put his arm around Benny and followed us. Figured.

I walked beside Thatch and Olivia was beside Benny. It was awkward, but I think only three out of the four of us knew that. Benny finally broke the silence, "So, Liv said she has a new job."

"What?" Thatch's head shot to her.

"Yeah. It's more just in the works. One of my old co-workers quit also and is starting his own firm and he wants me to work for him. It's still in the beginning phases, but when it's all up and running, I'll have a job. I'm helping him out with the set up now, though."

"Liv, that's awesome!" replied Thatch, moving to her and picking her up from behind in a bear hug.

"Yeah, congrats," I chimed in, although I had definitely already congratulated her when she got the news a week ago.

"Good. Well, I'm glad I don't have to worry about you as much anymore."

"No, big bro, you don't. I won't be living on the streets."

"Okay, but if you still need anything while this company is still taking off. I'm sure this guy can't really afford to pay you much right now."

"Seriously, you need to stop worrying about me," said Olivia. "I'm great. Better than great actually," she smiled.

"Well, good," he smiled back.

We headed to our separate vehicles and headed home. I beat Olivia there, mostly because she waited a few extra minutes to make sure Thatch wouldn't see her heading in the same direction as me.

"You had a good game too," she smiled when she walked into the living room and saw me waiting for her.

"I know. It was all because of you. I think the hypothesis has been thoroughly tested and you are, in fact, my good luck charm."

She sauntered over to me. "Maybe, or maybe it was because of this." She reached down and grabbed the hem of her jersey and pulled it off to reveal a tighter t-shirt jersey underneath with a new number and name on it; mine.

"What? When did you get this?"

"A couple of days ago. I couldn't go to the first home game since being married and not wear my new husband's number."

"Come here," I reached out a hand and lightly pinched the front of her shirt and pulled her closer to me. "This is quite possibly the hottest thing I've ever seen. I love you." A lot of girls have worn my name and number in the past, but it was nothing compared to this.

"I know. You're kind of obsessed with me."

"Hell yeah I am," I whispered into her lips before mine made contact with them.

Nights in with Olivia were my favourite. I loved playing hockey, I really did, but something changed in me where I found myself no longer craving the intensity of the game and longing to be on the ice. Now I was longing to be home with her, snuggled up on our couch watching a movie. Even when she did pick a boring *three-hour* long *classic*— and I actually mean classic. It was from nineteen-thirty-nine! I don't know why this Scarlett chick would ever want to be with a boring-ass, whiny man named Ashley, but for some reason, she was lovesick over him. And I'm sorry, but that chick got married *three times* throughout that entire movie. That's once per hour! Olivia also did point out the fact that

Ashley had blond hair and Rhett didn't (insert eye roll here). Her little theory may be true for movies, but she picked me in the end.

"Shhh, this is the best scene," she hushed me when I was about to say something. I watched quietly but had a hard time figuring out why that could possibly be her favourite scene.

"Are you kidding me? He just took advantage of her while he was drunk."

"No," she defended. "He swept her off her feet and carried her away up the staircase in a fit of passion. It's romantic."

"What the fuck is wrong with women?"

"Oh, shut up! See how happy she is the next morning. Because he rocked her world."

"You're so weird. Is that what you need? For me to be a bigger dick to you? Apparently that's what women want."

"Well, a bigger dick would be nice."

My face fell flat as I glared over at her. She could barely keep herself together because she knew damn well it wasn't true. "You're really proud of that one aren't you?"

She feverishly nodded while sucking her lips in, trying not to laugh. I pulled her down onto the couch and dragged her legs over to me so they were on either side of my hips and hovered over her, then I leaned down and captured her lips with mine. We weren't watching the rest of the movie and she was completely satisfied with my large appendage by the time I was done with her on that couch.

***

"That's it. I want a divorce!"

"Bullshit," I called back. "You'd never do all that paperwork."

"Nope, forget it; all of this. We can just pretend it never even happened and my brother will never know. It works out perfectly." Olivia headed for the stairs, but I caught up with her and grabbed her hand and pulled her back to me, kissing her the way she wanted. She pushed me off of her though. "You can't kiss me!"

"I can and I will. 'You should be kissed, and often, and by someone who knows how'." I think I delivered that line quite well, actually. Who knew quoting *Gone with the*

Wind was what I'd be doing on a Tuesday evening as a married man.

"Oh Jake," she threw her arms around me and kissed me harder. Then I scooped her up and carried her up the staircase to our bedroom.

"So, tell me," I began when I had her on the bed, "do I also get to be the first man to kiss you *all* over?" She nodded. "Fuck, I love you. This is the best night of my life." And I began kissing my way down her body until I was gently pulling up her little silk nightgown and kissing a path up her inner thigh getting closer and closer to where I wanted to be.

When we were done our little role play, we laid there under the covers facing one another. I gently played with her hair between my fingers as I was propped up on my forearm. I couldn't believe how much I loved this woman and every minute with her only made me want to do the selfish thing and keep her in that little bubble of ours forever, but I knew we couldn't do that. I knew we were going to have to break the news to everyone soon. We were both pretending like we had all the time in the world, but we knew it would all come crashing down eventually.

~ 19 ~

Olivia

I was sitting on the couch in the living room when Jake came in. He looked slightly panicked.

"You okay?" I asked him.

"Nope, sorry. I completely forgot that I'm having some of the guys from the team over tonight, so your brother is going to be here in about an hour."

"Oh, okay. I can go out then. I guess this was maybe going to happen eventually."

"No. I don't want to kick you out of our house. I can tell them something came up and I have to cancel."

"No, it's fine. I can leave," I tried to assure him.

"Liv, you're not going to leave all night."

"Well, how long are people going to be here for?"

"I have no idea. Given our track record, probably until after midnight at least. You can't stay out that late. You like to go to bed around eleven."

"Okay, well, I'll just hang out upstairs then. No one will even know I'm here."

"Are you sure about that?"

I nodded, "Yup. It's fine. I have some work to do for Henry and his new company and I can occupy myself until bed time. No one will suspect a thing."

"Okay, if you're sure."

"Yup," I smiled, giving him a quick kiss.

"Okay, thanks. I'm just going to go move the cars around so yours is hidden in the garage."

I could hear the party starting downstairs and I got a text from Greya asking if I was there and hiding. Our plan was working perfectly until I got unbearably hungry. I guess neither of us thought through the fact that I hadn't had dinner yet. I was still around when Jake was ordering pizza before people arrived, so I knew that was in the kitchen and it was tempting me. Would a girl risk it all for pizza? With every stomach growl, the answer was seemingly starting to move closer and closer to yes.

Me: *Do you think you can sneak up some pizza for me?*

Me: *Bring me food.*

Me: *Food.*

Why wasn't he answering?!

Me: *Your wife is starving!*

Me: *PIZZA!*

Me: *I will withhold sex!*

A few minutes later, the bedroom door opened and I saw Greya walking in with a plate in her hand.

"This is from your *husband*," she smiled.

Jake: *You better take that back!*

"Thank you," I smiled back, taking the plate from her. "How did you sneak up here?"

"They're all in the basement. I said I was going to the bathroom," she added while sitting on the bed across from me. "I will have to return soon though. But they may not actually notice I'm gone. The guys are all preoccupied watching a game and the wives/ girlfriends I can't be bothered to talk to. I mean, I will talk to them, I'm not mean, but it's very clear that some of them are only with some of the guys for the money. Should I tell Hollis his girlfriend is a gold digger?" I just smiled through my full mouth of pizza. "Maybe not, right?"

"Probably not," I replied once I had swallowed.

She sighed, "Oh well then."

"So, anything new in your life? You know all about the craziness over here, but I feel like I know nothing about you guys."

"Not really. Just the same old stuff. You getting used to Jake being gone a lot with away games?" Greya asked me.

"Yeah, it's okay. I miss him when he's gone, but it is getting easier. I'm getting used to it."

"Yeah, it definitely does get easier and before you know it, you'll love the break from him. I can have cereal for supper; it's great," she joked.

I finished my pizza while we chatted, but Greya eventually had to head back downstairs as to not draw any attention and I was left alone again. I fell asleep around eleven, as usual, but was awoken by Jake coming to bed.

"Hey," he whispered, pulling me into him. "Sorry about tonight, and thanks again for being so cool about it."

"No problem, but things like this are really starting to make me see that we need to tell people soon."

"I know. How about we go to my parents the next couple of days I have off and tell them? They have a few acres just outside of the city and I built a house for myself on their property so we can stay overnight."

"Yeah, that sounds nice."

***

We were headed out of the city to Jake's parent's place. They were only about an hour and a bit outside of the city, so it wasn't a far drive. I was looking forward to a little getaway with my husband, too. God, I will never get over calling him that. It was almost like a honeymoon; something he promised to take me on when the hockey season was done. I was sporting my new wedding band and Jake had his on too. I basically got to wear mine every day, but he didn't seeing as my brother would definitely notice something like that. I loved catching a glimpse of it on his finger. Who knew a piece of jewellery on a guy could be so hot?

When Jake pulled down the drive to his parent's place, it was a beautiful piece of farmland. I could imagine it in the summer with the horses running in the fields and our kids playing in the dirt—yeah, I couldn't wait to have kids with him. But I was still only twenty-five and we were going to wait a few years before that. Jake parked outside of the quaint guest house on their land. It was a modern-looking cabin that complemented the mountains off in the distance.

"It's freezing," I said, stepping out of the car.

"Well, it is December."

"Yes, but it seems colder here than back in the city."

"No, in the city you went from warm house to garage to car and never realized how cold it actually was." He came over and wrapped me in his arms, "But don't worry, I'll keep you warm."

We headed inside and dropped off our bags. Then we were back in the car and heading down the road to his parent's house.

"So, what exactly did you tell your parents when you said you were coming out here for a visit?"

"Not much. Just the usual, that I was going to stay at my place for a night and visit."

"So you didn't mention me?"

"I did say I was bringing someone with me, and my mom assumed it was a woman. I didn't give her the details, though."

"So…do you think they're going to be pleasantly surprised, just surprised, or upset and surprised?"

"Liv, I have no idea. But I do know that whatever their initial reaction is, they're going to love you by the end of this."

I stood on the porch of the massive farmhouse. It was gorgeous. Sure, I could try to come up with more or better words to describe it, but it was your typical beautiful farmhouse with rustic yet modern touches. Then the door finally swung open. My heart was pounding. I had no idea why I was so nervous, but I was. I guess I hoped they would like me—there was that people pleaser thing again. I never had in-laws before and I wanted to make a good first impression. Jake's brother was standing on the other side of the door.

"Hey man," greeted Jake when his brother finally looked up from his phone at him. He was seventeen and looked just like a younger Jake. The same dirty-blonde hair and stormy ocean eyes; tall with a muscular build. Even though they didn't have the same dad, their mom's genes must be the stronger ones, because Jake also looked a lot like his mother who was just walking down the front entryway to greet us. Her hair was lighter blonde though, and her eyes were this intense hazel.

"Whoa, dude," called his brother, slipping his phone into his pocket. "Who's this?" he glanced at me.

"This is Olivia," said Jake as we headed into the foyer and shut the door behind us.

His brother's eyes narrowed on me and I was slightly unnerved. "No, seriously. Who is this? You *never* bring girls here? I don't think we've ever met a girlfriend of yours since you were in high school—ow!" Jake's mom had given him a small smack on the back of the head.

"Be nice."

"I am being nice. I was just asking who she was."

"Hello, Olivia. It's nice to meet you," smiled Jake's mom. "I'm Caroline. You've already sort of met Cameron."

"It's nice to meet you," I smiled back. "You have a beautiful home, and this property is amazing."

"Well, thank you. We do love it out here. It's peaceful."

"Is Dad around?" asked Jake.

"He's around somewhere," replied Caroline. "I think he was in the garage earlier. But come in. Are you guys hungry? I can make some lunch."

"Sure, sounds good," replied Jake.

Jake's step-dad appeared while Caroline was making lunch and also seemed very taken aback by my presence. "Okay, your mom said you were bringing someone but I honestly didn't believe it until now." He smiled at me, "I'm Grant." Grant was a tall man with dark hair. He honestly looked like the odd one out of his family, and if I didn't know better, I'd question some things.

"Olivia, it's nice to meet you," I smiled.

"Gee, thanks Dad," added Jake. "Why is it so hard to believe that I could meet someone I would want to introduce you guys to?"

"Because you're you," mocked Cam.

"Okay, well...now that we're all here. I guess I may as well just tell you the reason we're here."

"Oh, she's pregnant, I knew it. Pay up, Dad," Cam motioned to his father and I couldn't help but laugh a little.

"Cameron!" scolded Caroline.

"She's not pregnant," assured Jake. "We're just uh...well...we're married. This is my wife."

Silence and wide eyes all around us.

"What?" Caroline finally broke the tension. "Are you serious?"

I couldn't tell if she was happy or upset. "Yes, I'm serious," nodded Jake, completely composed. "And this wasn't some sort of drunken mistake either. I am very much in love with this woman and married her because of it." He shot a glance at his brother, "On purpose."

A flat grin grew on his brother's face. "Well, damn, dude. Congrats!" called Cam, going in for a hug. Jake held his brother tight and soon I was met with my own from Caroline.

"Yay, I'm so happy to finally have a daughter-in-law."

"Um, thank you," I replied.

"Oh, thank God there will be another girl around at family events. I am seriously outnumbered by these three."

"I'm happy to be here," I smiled.

"I'm a little annoyed I didn't actually get a wedding out of this, but it's okay. I can forgive you," she added, going over to her son for a hug.

"Well, you never know. We might actually do the whole big wedding thing after the season is over," Jake assured her. We had never actually talked about if we should have any sort of elopement party—if that is what you would call it. Or maybe another wedding for our friends and family who missed the first one. I guess it only really hit me right in that moment that I missed out on getting to wear a wedding dress and have all of our family and friends celebrating with us. Huh? Maybe we would have to have a party someday.

"Welcome to the family," smiled Grant as he also hugged me, then his son. "We're happy to have you for as long as you'll put up with this guy." He then leaned closer to me and whispered, "Because I get it if you want to bail. He's a handful."

"Hey," shot Jake.

"But I love him anyway," he smiled.

"Yeah, I love him anyway, too. So I think you're stuck with me for a while," I added.

~ 20 ~

Jake

I could breathe a sigh of relief now. My family knew about Olivia, so one family down, only one more to go, and after seeing how happy my family was for us, I was starting to have some new hope that everything would be alright with Thatch. I hoped that my only saving grace in all of this would be the fact I married his sister and wasn't just fooling around with her, which was what he was afraid of.

"So, you're actually married," began Cam after dinner. My mom had made something that would rival some of the best rated restaurants in the city—as usual—and my brother and I were getting in some much needed bro time while Olivia chatted with my mom. "And she's not pregnant?"

"No. She's not pregnant. Stop asking me that." I killed his guy on the screen in front of us and we started a new game.

"Sorry. I mean, I'm stoked for you, don't get me wrong. And I'm thrilled to have a hot sister-in-law—"

"Hey," I playfully shoved him with my shoulder.

"But, I'm still just confused about how all of this happened."

"Well, she needed my help with a work thing and then I guess it started from there."

"Oh, so you guys knew each other already?"

"Um, well, sort of."

"Oh, I'm sensing something here. What does that mean?" He almost got me, but I managed to fire back at him and kill him again.

"Alright, she's…Thatch's sister."

"Ooh!" he put down his controller and looked at me. "How did he take that?"

"Well, he doesn't exactly know yet."

"What? Dude, you're screwed."

"I am not."

"Uh-uh. Bro code; don't go after your bro's sister."

"Grow up, will you. We're not in high school. I'm not just hooking up with her. I love her and I married her."

"Maybe, but still." We started yet another game. "Okay, just maybe wear a cup when you guys tell him," mocked Cam.

I smirked. That wasn't entirely a bad idea.

"So, have you applied for any colleges yet?" I changed the subject.

"A few," he shrugged. Cam was smart. Super smart, and he could honestly do anything he wanted to. He could easily go the med-school route like Dad, or engineering, or computer science stuff. He could become the next tech billionaire. The world was his oyster. "I just don't really know what I want to do. Dad is obviously pushing me into med-school, and it's not like I oppose the idea, but I just don't know if I really want that. Nothing speaks to me, though. How do they expect seventeen-year-old kids to just have their futures planned out after high school?"

"I don't know," I sighed. I guess I did luck out knowing hockey would be my career, but I still went to college and only got signed after that. "But I do know that you'll figure it out. You can always take some time off after you graduate. Travel or something."

"Yeah, Dad is not up for that."

"I'm sure we can convince him if that is really what you want. It'll all work out. Look at me. You think this is what I imagined my life to be like when I graduated high school?"

"An NHL star being paid millions and married to a younger hottie. Yeah, who would dream of that?"

"Okay, point taken. And she's only five years younger than me." Then said hottie walked into the room. "Hey," I smiled up at her.

"Hi," she greeted back and took the seat on the couch next to me.

"Have fun talking to my mom?" I asked.

"Yeah, she's great."

"She is. And she's super excited to have another girl in the family," added Cam. "I heard her talking to my dad while she was making dinner. She loves you already. It's kinda weird."

I smiled at that. "Well, how can you not love her?" I kissed her on the cheek.

"Aww," mocked Cam. "Okay, if you guys are going to be all lovey-dovey like this all the time, let me know now so I can steer clear." Then he shot up from the couch to his feet, "Yes! I finally killed you! Take that!"

I let my controller fall into my lap and slumped back farther into the couch. "Well, I was distracted."

"Yeah. You know, I might actually like having her around too."

***

"Hey," started Olivia when we were back at my guest house later that night. "Do you ever think about having an actual wedding? I never really did until your mom mentioned earlier how she was slightly disappointed to miss out on one."

"Yeah. I guess I never really thought about it before either. But if you want one, we can do that," I replied.

"Okay. I think maybe I would like to have some sort of celebration with all of our friends and family there."

"That would be nice. Once this is all out in the open and your brother can stand up there with me as my best man, we'll do this whole wedding thing right. It can even be as crazy and over-the-top as you'd like."

"Well, I don't know if I need that, but it sounds nice," she smiled, walking over to me and nestling herself against my chest for a hug. I wrapped my arms around her and let my chin rest on the top of her head. "So, what are the plans for tomorrow?" she looked up at me.

"I thought I'd take you riding."

"Wait. Actually, though?" she got all excited at the prospect of horseback riding. "Isn't it going to be cold?"

I shrugged. "The horses still need their exercise, and it's not that cold out. We'll dress warmly and we won't be out that long."

"Okay," she replied rather enthusiastically. "So, you're a cowboy too, then?" she added in a slightly mocking tone. "Damn, seriously," she shook her head.

"What?"

"You just really have the whole being every woman's fantasy thing down. It's kind of impressive."

"Yeah? So hockey player-cowboys are your thing?"

"Well, they never used to be, but we'll see how good you look on that horse tomorrow."

~ 21 ~

Olivia

Alright, I thought Jake looked sexy in his hockey stuff but that was before I had ever seen him in flannel and a cowboy hat. Was I a cowboy girl now? Probably, and him standing in the kitchen waiting for me looking all *rideable*, was causing some very real problems for me very fast.

"You ready to go?" he smiled at me when he noticed I was there.

"No, I think I choose to save the horse this time."

"What?" he cocked his head to the side.

"Come here," I motioned for him to come toward me. He put down his coffee mug and strode over to me. When he was close enough, I grabbed him by the flannel and took the hat on his head and placed it right onto mine. "I think I'd rather ride you first."

He understood me that time.

The weather was mild for early December and the ground was only lightly scattered with snow. We hadn't had any big snowfalls yet this year and I was thankful for it given my current position on top of a thousand pound animal. I was warmer than I thought I'd be while on our outdoor adventure. Jake's mom had lent me some winter riding pants and the fleece lining was doing wonders. We rode for about an hour and Jake led me to this beautiful clearing in the forest. We dismounted our horses and he pulled out a thermos of hot chocolate for us to enjoy while the horses were cooling down. He laid a blanket on a nearby fallen tree trunk and we sat there, huddled together.

I leaned my head on his shoulder. "This is really nice," I smiled. "Can we just stay here forever?"

"Well, maybe. But people might start to wonder why I left it all to live out here."

"Yeah, I guess," I stared off into the distance.

He wrapped his arm around me and pulled my chin upward to meet his gaze. "Everything is going to be fine. In a few weeks, I'll be sitting at your family's Christmas dinner and Thatch will be cracking jokes my way—about you, most likely, because he *will* be okay with this. In the end, he will see how much we love each other and how happy we both are. He ultimately only wants what's best for you and for you to be happy."

"How can you be so sure?"

"Because I know him. And you do too. I know you're scared because he's your big brother and you've looked up to him your whole life, and you have this overwhelming need to not disappoint him—or anyone—but I've known him for what? Only ten years less than you? And I know for a fact that he could never be disappointed by you."

***

We brushed the horses and fed them and headed back to Jake's guest house for a much needed shower. I let my hair fall out of my braid while standing before the bathroom mirror—man it smelled like horse. It's not like I rubbed my hair against the horse or anything, but somehow it took on all the horse essence just being in the same vicinity as the beast. Jake came up behind me, his cowboy hat and flannel already tossed to the side. He was just in his jeans and as he pulled my hair to the side and started kissing my neck, I could feel his strong bare chest against my back. He turned me quickly and just like our first shower encounter, he had my shirt off in record time and was lifting me onto the counter, nestling himself between my legs. He reached for my pants and just because that is how my cursed brain works, I grabbed his hand before he could also tear them off of me.

"Wait, it's weird. I'm wearing your mom's pants." His hand instantly froze and his face went flat as he stared at me—because only I could think of that in that particular moment and ruin it. "Sorry," I tried to backpedal, taking in his expression. He rested his forehead on mine and blew out a heavy breath. "Just don't think about it. I'll just go take them off, and put them far away from here," I added, jumping off the counter and heading out into the bedroom.

"Nope, you've ruined it. I will never now not think about taking off my mother's pants."

"Well, it's not like you're taking them off of her."

"Just stop talking," he pulled his hands to his face.

I came back into the bathroom a moment later, in just my underwear, but Jake was already in the shower. "Um, excuse me," I stood in front of the glass doors with hands fisted against my hips. He turned to look at me and a wicked smirk grew on his face. He tantalizingly slid the shower door open, just enough to reach a hand out and put it behind my neck, then pull me into the shower and press my warm, dry body against his wet, firm one. His lips captured mine with a hard, hungry kiss as he tore my remaining undergarments from me and let them fall, soaking wet, to the shower floor. He backed me against the tile wall and paused our frantic kiss for only a moment as he leaned down over me, water drowning his hair and streaming down his face. "So," I managed to get out in a whisper through heaving breaths, "are you going to turn up the heat?" I asked, remembering our first shower. His lips quirked into the most delicious smirk I have ever seen. Then he hoisted me up and my legs instinctively wrapped around his waist as he pushed his hips against me harder and captured my lips once again with a stomach flipping, smoulder inducing kiss. He moved us to the shower bench and sat on it all the while never breaking the contact of our lips. His fingers dragged through my wet hair, grabbing hold of it at the back of my head ensuring I couldn't break our contact even if I tried—not that I wanted to—while his other hand roamed my wet back and hips.

"Alright, I completely get the appeal of marriage now," he began in a low, heaving voice. "Getting to do this to you while calling you my wife, is probably the hottest fucking thing in the entire world."

I let out a small moan, "Well, say it again then."

He pulled my head closer to his and brought his lips a whisper away from my ear. "My wife," he growled.

He actually fucking *growled.*

And I melted.

~ 22 ~

Olivia

We got back from Jake's parent's place late that night. Jake was leaving the next morning for a couple of back-to-back away games and I was already starting to miss him. We knew that once he was back in the city, we were going to break the news to Owen. We couldn't keep this in anymore. The holidays were coming up and I realized that we needed to tell.

"Are you sure we want to do this today? Tomorrow might be better, or even sometime next week?" I said while I was parked on Owen's driveway.

"No," sighed Jake. "We have to. It's time."

"Are you sure you're ready to do this?"

"Yup," he smiled back at me. "I even wore a cup."

"What?" I glanced at his crotch.

"What? He's going to be pissed and I don't need him ruining his chances for any future nieces or nephews. He might actually like that one day."

"Oh my God," I rolled my eyes. "Okay, just let me go in there first and talk to them for a minute. I'll text you when you should come in."

"Alright," he said, giving me a salute with two of his fingers.

I got out of the car and walked slowly over to the front door. Owen didn't know I was coming over, but I had texted Greya ahead of time to make sure they were home. She answered the door and led me into the living room.

"Alright, babe," I could hear Owen calling from upstairs. "Laundry is done and you had better be waiting for me nake—AH!" he stopped on the stairs and looked at us. "Why is my sister here?"

"Gross," I called out.

"Shut up, I'm married," he called back, coming down the rest of the stairs and looking to Greya for answers.

"Oh, she just stopped by to tell us something. Some news of sorts."

"Oh, no. Is it about your new job?" asked Owen going to the kitchen.

"Um, no. That's all great."

"Then what is it?" he asked.

"Uh…okay…" I took a deep breath.

"What is it, Liv?" Owen was starting to sound worried and slightly agitated.

"It's nothing bad. Well, not to me." He stared at me. There were only a few times in my life when I was terrified to tell my big brother something and this was very quickly shooting to the top of the list. "So, I've actually been seeing someone for a bit now and a couple of months ago we were in Vegas, and…"

"Spit it out, Olivia!" urged Owen sounding slightly displeased.

"I sort of…got married."

"What?! What the actual fuck, Olivia!" shouted Owen. "You've been married for a couple of months and didn't tell us? Why would you do this?" He paused. "If you tell me that you're pregnant I'm going to lose my mind."

"I'm not pregnant."

"Well, then. Who is this guy?"

"He's in my car. I want you guys to meet him."

"Great! Bring him inside," he motioned toward the door.

I shot Greya a quick look and texted Jake. She immediately turned to Owen and he looked completely taken aback at her sudden change in demeanour and what was happening. "Okay, you listen to me and you listen *very* carefully," she began in this quiet, terrifying voice. Honestly, I was scared of her in that moment so I could only imagine what my brother was feeling. "If you so much as blink the wrong way when she opens that door and you see who is on the other side of it, you will be sleeping in the guest room for the next few months. And you will become *very* comfortable with your own company, do you hear me?"

He stared at her. "Wh—who is on the other side of that door?! What do you know, woman?!"

"Someone your sister loves very much and who loves her back, so you don't get a say in it."

He crossed his arms and pursed his lips. "Yeah, and did you think your little punishment through given our current situation?"

She paused. "Well, I guess that's just on hold then. Or, I will allow one conjugal visit per month and that is it. Maybe two."

He rolled his eyes.

"What?" I interrupted. "Am I going to be an aunt? I mean, gross, but yay!"

"Well, not yet anyway," added Greya.

There was a knock at the door and we all turned in that direction. I took a deep breath and walked, what felt like a thousand steps, to the door. I let Jake in and we slowly walked out of the foyer and into the kitchen.

"OH. FUCK. NO!" called out Owen when we came around the corner.

"I warned you!" yelled Greya, and she pushed him past us and up the stairs.

We could hear them arguing, but couldn't make out anything they were saying. It went on for about ten minutes where Jake and I just sat on the couch waiting for them to return.

"It's okay, I think Greya's calming him down," I finally said.

"Yeah. She's going to be taking a lot of shit for this too, though."

"He loves her. He's not going to stay mad at her."

"Same as he loves you," Jake squeezed my hand. "It's me he's going to hate."

Then we looked up. We could hear them walking down the stairs. Greya was first, with Owen trailing behind looking ready to interrogate the hell out of us. He sat across from us and menacingly stared at Jake. Then glanced at me.

"How the fuck did this happen?" he asked in a scarily calm tone.

"Well, he was helping me with something for work, and then I guess it started from there," I replied.

He then turned to Jake. "So she's the girl you've been hung up on for the last few months?"

"Yup."

"And not once did you think to tell me!"

"Well, dude, come on. What would you have done?"

"Punched you."

"Yeah, and that wouldn't have helped anything. We decided to wait and see where things went until we told you."

"And apparently it went *down the aisle!* What the fuck were you two thinking? Wait…did this happen after the Vegas game a couple of months ago?"

"Yeah," I guiltily chimed in.

"She was in Vegas with us?! Fuck, dude! You not only dated my sister behind my back, but married her too! That's not cool."

"You know what? You're sounding like a bit of a hypocrite," responded Jake.

Owen's head snapped back and he glared at him. "*What?*"

"I seem to remember you saying you wouldn't go for Gabe's cousin because she was basically his sister."

"That was different. I didn't date her behind his back and marry her. We were friends first and everyone knew about it!"

"I mean, it's similar…" added Greya.

"You are on *very* thin ice with me too right now," he shot back at her.

She rolled her eyes and he turned back to us but I cut him off before he could say more. "Look, this isn't like we got drunk in Vegas and got married. We love each other and want to spend the rest of our lives together."

"How can you know that after a few months?"

"You just can," added Jake. "Once you actually started dating Benny how long did it take you to know she was it for you?" Owen didn't answer. He just kept staring us down, breathing ominously. I kept waiting for him to lunge at Jake and start kicking his ass. Then Jake stood. "Look, Thatch. I love your sister more than anything and I never in a million years thought I would get married and find that kind of love. I would never hurt her or do anything to make her upset. You know me. Do you actually think I wouldn't treat her the way she deserves? She is the best person I know, and she made me feel what it's like to have someone love you in spite of all your faults and love me for me and not just the money or anything else. You yourself said whoever this girl was that had me all in love was lucky because I'm one of the best guys you know."

Owen took a deep breath and stood too. This was it. He was going to punch Jake. *I wonder what it's like to be a hockey widow?* Greya and I watched, frozen in place.

Jake flinched slightly when Owen walked up to him. "If you ever so much as make my sister shed a single tear over you, I will kick your ass so hard that you will never play hockey again."

"Got it," he replied.

They eyed each other up for a moment, then Owen swung the arm at his side and—"Ah! What the fuck, dude? Are you wearing a cup?" he held his hand with the other.

"Uh, yeah."

Then Owen laughed. I couldn't believe he was actually laughing. Greya and I exchanged a glance and I breathed a sigh of relief.

"Alright, I guess let's celebrate or whatever," said Owen, heading to the liquor cabinet.

"Are you okay?" I asked Jake.

"Yup, I'm good," he smiled.

I looked over at Owen and Greya, who was trying to kiss him, but he was still pissed at her too. They were pretty cute. He was trying to avoid her advances and she wasn't giving up. They were both laughing and he finally picked her up and put her on the kitchen counter and kissed her. I hoped that years from now, Jake and I were still that much in love. But I think the chances were pretty good.

~ 23 ~

Jake

The holidays came and went and I loved getting to spend them with Olivia and her family and then mine. Thatch had warmed up to the idea of us and even helped soften the blow with his parents when we announced that we were married at Christmas dinner.

***

"Sup, bro?" greeted Thatch when he arrived for our next home game.

"Hey," I nodded toward him.

"Or I guess I should say bro-in-law now." He shook his head, "That's still so weird to me. But I guess it's a good thing. She's your problem now. No refunds or returns. Remember that. Good luck, bro."

"Hang on," interrupted Hollis. "What did you just say?" he turned to Thatch and then back to me. "Did you marry his sister?!"

"Uh," I reached a hand behind my neck and scratched it, "yeah."

The entire locker room fell silent.

"Wait, wait, wait, hang on. What?!" Nyles interrupted. "And you're still breathing?!"

"Alright, guys. Yes. I did get married and I would have announced it to everyone sooner, but there were some things needing to be worked out. I did, in fact, marry Thatch's sister and yes, I'm still *breathing*," I glanced at Nyles. "He's not going to kill our best player," I mocked.

"Holy shit, dude!" called Hollis. "Well, congrats I guess! Who would have thought that out of all of us, Ellis would be the one to bag the untouchable Olivia Thatcher."

"Alright, enough. That's my sister, and while I would have kicked any one of your asses for looking at her, I'm sure Ellis feels pretty strongly about any of you looking at his *wife*."

"Point taken," agreed Hollis. Then he smiled and clapped me on my back, "But congrats again man. That's awesome."

We won that game and when I slid into bed that night next to Olivia after my whole team supported me in my marriage, I couldn't imagine it getting any better than that.

The next few months with Olivia were even better than before. Now that everyone knew about us, I didn't have to hide my excitement about seeing Thatch's sister after our games. She was waiting with Benny outside of the locker room after our last home game and I headed straight for her and picked her up and pressed her against the wall and kissed her. Her legs wrapped around my waist as one of my hands grabbed the back of her head and tugged at her hair.

"Okay, I might be cool with this now, but can you at least go somewhere else?" interrupted Thatch. We turned to see him standing there with an arm over Benny. I placed his sister nicely back on the ground and we headed over to where they were standing.

"So, you guys ready for this?" asked Olivia. "Only one more game to the playof—"

I immediately clasped my hand over her mouth and pulled her into me. "Shh. Don't mention it."

"Yeah, what have you been teaching your wife?" questioned Thatch. "You're going to jinx it."

Benny was just rolling her eyes at the conversation.

Olivia wriggled free, "I am not. But fine. I won't acknowledge the elephant in the room."

"Good girl," I smiled and kissed her on the top of her head.

We made it to the playoffs—despite Olivia's almost jinxing. The last few months with Olivia had been the best months of my life and now that we were so close to the Cup, I could just feel it; this was our year.

I was away a lot, though, with all the games, and when I was home, Olivia and I were starting to fall into a routine of just seeing each other in passing. She was busy helping Henry get his new company going and she now had a regular work schedule and was working five days a week and sometimes putting in a few extra hours on the weekend—I loved her for her work ethic, but selfishly I was starting to miss my unemployed wife that was always around. She was happier than ever though, and hearing her talk about work and seeing her face light up when she did, made all the time apart worth it.

I came home after practice to find Olivia baking in the kitchen. She had Spice Girls blaring through the sound system and was mixing what looked like chocolate cake batter.

"Hi," I smiled at her.

"Hey," she smiled back.

"What are you doing?"

"Baking. What does it look like I'm doing?"

I folded my arms against my chest and leaned a hip against the counter. "I can see that. I mean why? Not that I don't love coming home to the idea of chocolate cake."

She shrugged, "I don't know. I just felt like it. Want to lick the beater?" she held one up to me.

"Yeah. And then I want to lick something else," I held her gaze as I took the batter-covered beater from her.

She let out a groan that Marge Simpson would be proud of and rolled her eyes, "Why is it that you can always make something into something dirty?"

"All guys can. It's just how our brains work."

"Whatever." She moved to the oven and opened it, bending down and sliding the cake pan in, giving me an impressive angle of her perfect ass covered just enough by the little sundress she was wearing.

"Well, I'm not the one walking around the house looking like that."

She stood. "Yeah, that'd be weird if you were wearing a dress," she smirked.

"Uh-huh. Well, that dress is doing things to me," I swiped my tongue over the beater.

"Yes. I have heard that the sundress is to guys what grey sweats are to girls. I don't get it, but whatever," she shrugged.

"Grey sweats don't make any sense. A sundress makes perfect sense; it's easy access."

"Oh my God," she just rolled her eyes at me.

"Get over here," I demanded, motioning for her and tossing the licked-clean beater into the sink.

***

Olivia was soaking in the tub when I walked in with a piece of chocolate cake for her.

"Mmm," she smiled. "I did pick a good one. Girls, marry the guy who will bring you chocolate cake while in a bubble bath. That should be the new standard."

"Hate to break it to you, GT, but that's not a very high standard. One: a guy will use any excuse to walk into the bathroom while his girl is naked in the tub. And two," he paused a moment, "okay, maybe there isn't a two."

She just laughed through a mouthful of cake. "You might think so, but it's actually surprising how little effort guys will put in and how much girls will let them get away with it."

"Well, that's sad then. This was basically zero effort for me."

***

We were two games away from making it to the Cup and needless to say, Thatch and I were *slightly* stressed over it. I mean, we had this, but we couldn't get cocky about it. We had made it that far before, only to have it taken from us. The night before we flew out for our next game, Thatch had us over for dinner. I think that was the first time I had dinner at their place with Olivia. It was slightly weird, standing on his front step, seeing as the last time I was there we were telling him that I married his sister and I figured it would be my last day on earth. Benny answered the door and we headed into the kitchen where Thatch was seasoning some steaks for the grill.

"Need help with anything?" asked Olivia as she put the bottle of wine we brought on the counter.

"I think we're good. I'm just going to go grill these," answered Thatch. "Wanna come?" he asked me.

I nodded and we headed for the deck while Benny poured a drink for Olivia and they chatted about whatever it was they were chatting about.

"So," began Thatch as he opened the grill and started placing slabs of meat on it. "How are things?"

I don't know why, but his question seemed odd to me. Forced or something, or slightly awkward. "Fine," I shrugged. "Why are you asking it like that?"

"I don't know. Because it's still kinda weird that you're married to my sister and me asking you how things are also implies that I'm asking how things with you guys are and on the one hand, I don't really want to know about your love life with my sister, but on the other hand, I do. You know?"

"Not really? But things are good," I smiled.

"Oh, hang on," he added, slipping a hand into his pocket and pulling out his phone. He handed it over to me, "Can you take a quick picture?"

"Uh, sure."

"Gabe sent me a photo this morning of Elsie's Ken doll barbequing with a tiara on and the caption said 'If you're not barbequing with a tiara, you're doing it wrong,'. It's also a running joke between us because she insists the doll is me because it does strangely look like me. It's weird. So…" He also pulled a plastic tiara from behind the grill and placed it on his head. He looked utterly ridiculous, but damn, was there anything he wouldn't do for that kid? It made me feel good knowing he'd most likely be like that with my kids one day.

I snapped the pic and handed his phone back. "You really do way too much for that kid," I mocked.

"I know. It is a problem. But I physically can't stop myself."

I grinned, "I guess it's nice to know you'll be a great uncle to my kids too one day. Not that I had any doubts." He shot me a terrified look. "Not now. Why does everyone keep thinking Olivia's pregnant?"

"Because you got married out of the blue. But anyway, I *will* be an amazing uncle one day. And you will be too," he clapped a hand on my shoulder as he flipped the steaks. "You ready for tomorrow?"

"Fuck, I thought we weren't going to bring it up?"

"It's just another game. Nothing different than the last," he said so casually. I don't know how he did it. I liked to act cool and arrogant most of the time—I will admit that—but when you get this close to victory, it's hard not to let doubt wriggle its way in. "Okay, these are done," he said, taking the steaks off the grill and putting them on a new plate. "Let's go see what the ladies have been up to."

We headed inside and Thatch placed the tiara on Olivia as he walked past her. "What?" she questioned, taking it off her head.

"Don't ask," I replied, walking past her.

"Is that from my bachelorette party?" Benny added.

Dinner was great and for a moment I had completely forgotten that in a few hours I would be on a plane. I had done this many times in my life but the feeling is never lost on me that this could finally be the year we make it. I know it's the nature of the game that one team has to lose for the other to win, and making it that far still says something about your team, but it doesn't make the loss sting any less.

Wifey: *Good luck tonight *kissy face emoji* Whether you win or lose, I'll still be here waiting for you when you get home…in our bed…and I may have gone shopping earlier *winky face emoji**

Me: *God I love you.*

Wifey: *I know.*

Me: *Thanks though. I hate to admit it, but I'm a bit nervous.*

Wifey: *What? You?*

Me: *I know right?*

Wifey: *You've got this. Just do what you do best.*

Me: *I can't fuck you on the ice *winky face emoji**

Wifey: *Okay, that other thing you do best.*

Me: *Got it.*

There was a knock on my hotel room door. I stood from the edge of the bed and sauntered over there, pulling the door open when I reached it.

"You ready?" asked Thatch.

"More than you know."

~ 24 ~

Olivia

Holy crap! They made it to the Stanley Cup final game. I had only been hearing about this day from my brother since he was signed by Colorado, but now that my husband was also on the team, it meant so much more to all of us. Greya and I were sitting in the arena before the game.

"Shit," started Greya. "I'm actually really nervous. I know I've been teasing Owen for the last few years about making it to the Cup, but now that it is actually happening, I don't know what to do with myself."

"Yeah. They've got this, though. They made it this far."

"I guess, but—no, I'm not going to think about it," she gave her head a slight shake and smiled at me. "I've been in this position before, a few times actually, with my dad. I mean, it's not like I ever wanted my dad to lose, but for some reason I'm way more invested this time than I ever was before. I really want them to win."

"Mostly because they'll both be complete sourpusses for about a month after this if they don't," I joked.

"Well, yeah, there's that, too."

"Hey guys," interrupted Stella. She was making her way to our seats with a baby strapped to her chest and Gabe following her with their daughter, Elsie in hand.

"Hey," Greya smiled back as they took their seats.

"Shit, I'm so nervous," started Gabe.

"Okay, well, we can't *all* be nervous for them," replied Greya, her wavering voice coming through. "Some of us should know they've got this."

"Oh, yeah, they've totally got this," answered Stella with an air of certainty while she placed a pair of baby noise cancelling headphones on the nine-month-old. "I can feel it, and I'm usually pretty good with things like this."

"She is," nodded Gabe. Then he turned to Elsie, "Is Uncle Owen going to win the Cup tonight?"

"But we have cups at home," she replied and we all smiled.

"This is a special cup you get if you're the best hockey team out of all the hockey teams and Uncle Owen really wants it."

"Oh, okay. Then yes! He's going to get that cup!"

"That's the spirit," cheered Gabe.

I turned my attention back to the ice and looked for Jake out there. I finally spotted him next to my brother as they were waiting for the game to start.

That was the longest hockey game of my life. It was tied four-four and we were down to the final three minutes. We all desperately didn't want it to go into overtime. I glanced over at Greya for a second and she was on the edge of her seat—literally. Then her eyes shot to something and I followed her gaze. Jake had a breakaway and that was it. We all collectively stood and watched as he neared the other team's net. And as if time slowed, it happened. I was only broken from my trance by the sound of the goal and the crowd's cheers around us, pulling me back to reality.

They did it.

They won!

I got this overwhelming urge to just run onto the ice and leap into Jake's arms. But I didn't. I mean, I couldn't exactly do that. I had to settle for Greya when we simultaneously looked at each other and embraced.

"Holy shit!" she called out, bouncing up and down in my arms.

"I know! I have no idea what to do now or how to feel."

"Me too."

The team was presented with the Cup and Elsie was definitely in awe with it and agreed that it was much cooler than any cup they had at home. When we finally did get the chance to see Owen and Jake after the game, I had never seen either of them happier than they were in that moment. I mean, they both married the loves of their lives that year, but apparently this was better? I will never fully understand men. I won't take any offence to it either.

Jake was being interviewed and I was standing off to the side waiting for him to be done. I could hear everything he was saying and the questions the interviewer was asking, but I honestly kind of zoned out for most of it, just in awe of that man being my husband, but I was brought back with her next question.

"So, what does the celebration look like for you tonight? We all know you know how to party," the interviewer asked.

"Oh, man," Jake began. "I don't know. I don't think the celebration is going to be too wild tonight. I'm probably just going to have a night in celebrating with my wife."

The interviewer's eyes widened as she composed herself to respond. "I'm sorry, I think I misheard you. Did you just say, 'your wife'?"

"Sure did. Going on eight-ish months or so. So I'll probably just be celebrating with her and Thatcher and his wife. Maybe a couple of other teammates." He was so casual about it and I loved him for that. He knew he just dropped on a bomb on the Jake Ellis fan community, but he didn't care.

Her eyes never went back to their normal size. "Wow, okay. Well, I'm sure a lot of hearts are breaking right now, but congrats again on the win...and the wedding I guess."

"Thanks," he flashed her that classic Jake Ellis smile.

My brother came up behind him and wrapped him in a bear hug and kissed him on the cheek. "This is my brother-in-law, and the best guy I know." God, you'd think he was drunk the way he was acting.

"Wait," began the interviewer again. "You married his sister?"

"Sure did," Jake smiled again. Then he turned and found me off to the side and took the few steps over to me and pulled me into him, kissing me hard and without restraint.

"Dude, what have I told you about doing that in front of me," Owen called over to us.

"I don't care, man. We just won the Cup!"

"Hell yeah, we did!" he called back. "So, worth delaying our honeymoon for?" Owen asked Greya.

"I mean, I guess," she mocked, then he bent down and picked her up and kissed her.

Jake turned and smiled down at me and did the same. I was in heaven, feeling like the only girl in the entire world.

So this is what it's like to be married to a Stanley Cup champion.

Holy crap, that was a weird thing to say.

The celebration that night consisted of a lot of alcohol and *a lot* of other things. You'd think that man would be tired after playing a hockey game, but the win only seemed to give him more energy.

Our hotel room bed was a mess of sheets for most of the night after we returned from the celebration in Owen's room. It was just the eight of us: me, Jake, Owen, Greya, Stella, Gabe and their two kids, after the big team celebration was over. We were drinking and laughing and living in the moment. I don't think it fully hit any of us that they had won. We all knew it, but it was surreal to the max.

~ EPILOGUE ~

Olivia

Jake and I finally did decide to have an actual wedding. It may have been a long time coming, but it was finally my wedding day—well, second wedding day. The first never really felt like it, seeing as it was more of a spur-of-the-moment decision. Greya helped me into my off the shoulder, colourfully floral embellished—because I felt slightly weird wearing all white seeing as I was already married and a little bit of colour suited me and our wedding well—wedding dress that cost more than a dress should, but Jake insisted on me getting the one I loved. I would have married him in a paper bag though, and let's face it, he probably wouldn't have complained about that. He'd say something dumb like, 'at least it would rip off of you easily'.

"You look amazing," Greya smiled. "Jake's a lucky guy."

"Oh, he knows it," I smiled back. "I'm lucky too though."

"See, I told you to bang the hockey player," added Keira after a sip of champagne.

We headed out into the hallway of the venue and I found my brother waiting there. "Wow, Liv," he gave me a once over. "You look amazing."

"Thank you," I smiled back.

"Ellis is just out there," he pointed behind him, "waiting for that whole first look thing with your photographer."

"Thanks." I turned to Greya. "I'll come find you after," I told her.

"Yup," she nodded.

I headed out of the glass doors onto the patio where Jake was waiting. He was standing with his back to the door looking out at the gardens below, where our ceremony would take place. We had booked this gorgeous estate with a garden made for weddings.

"Hey," I called out to him, and he turned at the sound of my voice. Damn he looked sexy in a tux. I'm not sure which version of him I liked better: hockey player, cowboy, or all formal and suave looking. He rocked all of them and just knowing that he was mine and I got to be the one to call him that, made my heart flutter.

"Holy fuck," his eyes widened and raked over me, causing an instant flush of heat throughout my veins. "Damn." He walked over to me and took my hands in his. "I mean you were gorgeous the day I married you, but this is something else. We should have weddings more often," he joked.

"I don't think you can afford to marry me again every year."

"I don't care. I will marry you again, and again, and again, every year for the rest of my life." He leaned down to kiss me. It wasn't hard or fast or laced with unbridled passion. It was slow and soft and full of the love that we shared for one another.

"Alright, you two," called the photographer. "I think that's all I need and it's time for the ceremony."

"Thanks," I turned to look at her.

I walked down the aisle with my arm linked through my brother's. He was still Jake's best man, but he was serving double duty and also giving me away which meant more to the both of us than he probably realized. This was the moment we had been waiting for since we got married the first time. All of our family and friends were there and my brother was proudly standing by Jake's side once we had made it to the altar.

Our ceremony was short and sweet, seeing as we had already been legally married for a while now. Just some vows and a stand-in officiant that didn't need any real authority. The party was what we were really after and the night was honestly better than I had ever dreamed it could be. I danced with my husband all night under the blanket of stars and twinkling lights.

Jake held me in his arms until I awoke the next morning to the feeling of utter and complete bliss. Just like he said, I would marry him over and over again, too.

"Good morning," I heard him whisper in my ear as he pulled me closer to him.

"Good morning," I said with a smile back. "So, was last night everything you imagined it would be?"

"Yes, but also better," he replied while gently twirling the diamond ring on my finger. "Should we go get some breakfast or stay in bed longer?"

I pondered a moment. "Can we do both? I think breakfast in bed sounds great."

"Sure," he smiled, moving to the nightstand to look through the room service menu. "Whatever my wife wants."

"Oh, say that one more time," I seductively teased.

"My wife."

Jake

A couple of months after our wedding, Olivia and I had returned home from our honeymoon. We had an amazing time in the Maldives, and I loved the fact that her attire every day was pretty much just a bikini and I never had to waste time undressing her if I wanted her.

"Hey," she called from the top of the stairs, "You okay if Greya and Owen stop by? They want to see us now that we're back."

"Yeah, sure," I called back.

About forty minutes later, Benny and Thatch were at our door and I was inviting them in.

"Hey guys," called Benny, pulling Olivia into a big hug. "How was the honeymoon?"

"It was great," Olivia replied. "I wish we didn't have to come home."

"Yeah, I get that," she smiled back.

We headed into the living room and sat on the couch. "So, how have you guys been?" I asked.

"Uh, pretty good," began Thatch.

"Oh, we found out we're having a boy," Benny casually slipped in.

"What?!" Olivia shot to her feet. "Oh my God! You're pregnant?!" she practically yelled at Benny.

"Yup," she smiled back.

I looked at Thatch, "No way, man. Congrats!"

"Oh, my God!" Olivia said again and finally managed to sit back down. "I'm going to be an aunt. I can't believe this. And a boy…"

"Yeah," Benny smiled back.

"Wait, how far along are you then?" Olivia asked.

"Only the first trimester. We did that early genetic testing shit because Owen is a worrywart and wanted to know if there was any chance of anything we'd need to prepare for in the future. So, they say it's a boy, but I guess we'll get it confirmed at the anatomy ultrasound next month."

"Oh my God. Well, either way, I'm so excited."

"Yeah, we can tell," smiled Owen.

"Have you thought of names yet?" Olivia just had question after question ready in the barrel.

"Not really," replied Benny.

"Yeah, well. We all know I get to name him. You suck at naming things," mocked Thatch.

I dragged Thatch to the basement while the girls talked baby stuff upstairs, and poured us each a glass of whiskey. "Holy shit, dude. You're going to be a dad," I said, clinking my glass against his.

"I know, right?" He sounded slightly nervous.

"Hey, you are going to be the best dad in the entire world," I reassured him. "Just look at you and Elsie."

"I know. But at the end of the day, she's not my kid."

"That's how I know you'll be an amazing dad. Because just imagine what you'll be like with your own kid."

"Yeah, I guess."

They left a couple of hours later and it was just Olivia and me sitting on the couch. She was leaning against me with one of her knees pulled up to her chest as I slowly dragged my fingers through her hair. "Well, that was crazy," she began. "I did not expect them to tell us that when they came over."

"Yeah," I agreed, although I figured they'd be announcing something like that soonish seeing as they had been apparently trying for the last couple of years. Who knows what that really entailed though, as I don't really care to know the ins and outs of my friends' sex lives. Maybe they put the baby thing on hold for a while after we won the Cup. Either way, I was stoked for them and it made me think about Liv and I's future as well. "You think that'll be us one day?" I asked.

She raised her head from my shoulder and looked back at me with that bratty look I both loved and hated. "So…this is when I tell you I'm also pregnant, right?"

"Don't even joke with me, love."

"It's not a joke." I froze, but then her smile gave it away. "Okay, fine. I'm just kidding."

"You're such a brat."

"But I do think that will be us eventually. Maybe not anytime soon, but definitely one day."

"One day sounds perfect. In the meantime, we can get a lot of practice in." How was I not going to make that joke? Come on.

"Mmmhmm," she groaned and leaned her head back on my shoulder as I stroked a finger up and down her exposed thigh. "You noticed I'm wearing a sundress?" she asked.

"Oh yeah, I noticed."

"Well, are you going to do anything about it?" I glanced down at her. "You know, the easy access and all. You can fu—"

"Language, good girl," I playfully scolded her.

She moved to my lap and laced her fingers behind my neck. "I'm not that much of a good girl."

"Oh, you're definitely still a good girl. But you're *my* good girl."

"Yeah I am. For life, baby," she wiggled her ring finger in front of me.

I took her hand in mine, "For life." I kissed the ring and her hand, "And every lifetime after."

Want More?

Check out Owen and Greya's story if you haven't already.
Book 1 in the Mile High City Series:

Between Awake and Sleep

and

Book 2, Stella and Gabe's story:

The Stella Problem

Follow on Instagram: **@a.louiseauthor**

About the Author

Alexandra Louise lives in Alberta, Canada with her husband and daughters. She spends most of her time writing and taking care of her littles because she enjoys being bossed around by tiny dictators, retreating to her own fictional worlds, and getting paid for neither. Her books are full of relatable characters, fun adventures, low spice/ fade to black for everyone to enjoy, swoony moments, and of course happily-ever-afters.

Other Titles by Alexandra Louise:

Fantasy Romance:

The Snow Thief (Book 1)

The Queen's Return (Book 2)

Novellas:

Save a Horse

Knot Your Average Holiday

Mile High City Series

Between Awake and Sleep (Book 1)

The Stella Problem (Book 2)

Off-Limits (Book 3)